Ken Lansdowne

Dance: Ten Murder: Maybe?

A Bent Mystery

5

H Publishing

Dedicated To:
To all the missing people that once filled my life.
You were taken to soon and are missed and remembered.

Copyright © 2012 by Ken Lansdowne.
Publisher: H Publishing
          605 Clinton Street,
          Denver, Colorado 80247.

PUBLISHERS NOTE: This is a work of
fiction. Names, characters, and incid-
ents are the product of the authors imagination or are used fictitiously. Any res-
emblance to actual persons living or
dead, or events are entirely coin-
cidental.

First Printing: 2012

Library of Congress Cataloging in Publication Data
    Dance: Ten, Murder: Maybe? : A Bent Mystery: a novel/
Ken Lansdowne
        p.   cm.
    ISBN 0-9740853-0-8/978-0-9740853-0-2
    1. Title

Printed in USA   H Publishing

OTHER BOOKS BY THE AUTHOR

Jacob Marley
A Victorian Novella

THE BENT MYSTERY SERIES:
Secrets Don't Belong In Closets
A Murderous Ball Of Fluff
The Fairy Dust Killer
Home Sweet Homo
A Mystery Wrapped In A Mystery
Surrounded By A Mystery
The Art Of Death

◆◆◆◆◆◆◆◆◆◆◆◆◆◆◆◆◆◆◆◆◆◆◆◆◆◆

Dance: Ten

Murder: Maybe?

One

 "And this, fellow visitor..."

Len Matthews was doing one of his more annoying bits, acting as a tour guide pointing out the oddities populating the area he and JB were walking in. It was the deluxe Gay Line tour showing off the Upper Westside of Manhattan. Interesting, since JB (Jeremy Bent to his fans. As a well selling mystery novelist he did have a few) and Len (Yes, that would be *the* Len Matthews. Star of the Broadway stage, a cabaret performer, and, just lately (further inflating an already overblown ego according to JB) he had been a guest star on two national TV series that were then shooting in New York. And, oh yes, in case it wasn't clear, JB's best friend.

Anyway, to return to the point, both JB and Len lived on the Eastside of the same city. It wasn't as if they needed a passport to get across Central Park. So Len's suto tour was silly and unnecessary, but typical of him and his sometimes warped sense of fun. And he wouldn't stop.

"Look at them," Len kept on. "There. Straight ahead. Now, that is a prime example of what I'm saying. Observe. A perfect Westside cliché couple." He put a palm on JB's chest. "Be careful. Don't make a noise. You don't want to make them skitter away. They frighten easily."

Len was indicating a gay couple walking toward them on Columbus Avenue. Columbus was one of the busier thoroughfares in good old New York. The two men Len was pointing at were walking close, their arms around each other, laughing together. This was something gay couples did all the time in the city. Even then, at the end of Nineteen-eighty-six, it still wasn't the norm, but gays could get away with it in New York. Out in the boondocks of America it would have been pretty scandalous. In New York? Just another couple. Mostly unnoticed. Except by Len.

JB had to admit that Len had a point. They were what was called in Gayspeak "clones". One of the men was dressed in a black leather motorcycle jacket, with a silver cockring displayed under the shoulder epaulet, a pair of 501 jeans, and tan work boots. The other had on an Air Force olive sage green jacket with a bright orange lining, made of padded nylon. He had an identical pair of jeans as his partner, but with white socks and brown penny loafers.

JB turned to Len. "Does it occur to you that they might be thinking something similar about us?" The two men passed by Len and JB giggling and whispering God knew what..

"Nonsense!" Len tended to exclaim a bit when in the midst of proving a point. "A bonified Eastsider will fit in anywhere. A Westside clone in that uniform over at Charlie's? He'd stand out like a cheerleader at a funeral. No, those boys were far too rough, too underdressed for Charlie's."

Len was referring to one of the better known gay bars on New York's Upper Eastside. A restaurant and bar combined, located on First Avenue, at a convenient corner in the mid Twenty's. It could boast a nice after work crowd most weekday evenings. Which meant business suits and wing-tips were the usual uniform of its habitués. JB and

2

Len had spent a few happy hours there over the years.

Usually JB would take exception to many of Len's theories, but in this case even JB could see the point Len was trying to make.

"All right, I get it. You mean, it's as if an Eastsider was found at Pamplona in May?"

Len raised an eyebrow.

"The Run For The Bulls? Hemingway." He ran his hand up and down his chest. "Suit and tie out of place?"

"Exactly!"

JB and Len were, that October morning, at JB's insistence, having their Saturday brunch at one of the numerous cafes situated there on the Westside Avenue. JB had claimed to be bored with their usual place located down the street from their apartment building over on East Sixty-fourth. He believed it would do both of them some good to see another part of the city.

The area that stretched from the Columbus Avenue ABC studios at around Sixty-third to the East Side bus crossover over at Central Park, in the Eighty's, had become a very chic place to visit in the last few years. Broadway, only a block over, was too business oriented to be interesting or trendy. Columbus and Amsterdam Avenues, which ran parallel to Broadway, had developed into boutiques, antique shops, and clothiers in charming store fronts, one after another. Block after block. There was also a deli or two mixed in, several Korean groceries, and, on Columbus, one or two gay bars to fill in between the expensive custom shops. One of the reasons JB had wanted to explore this stretch of Columbus was an article in that mornings *Times*. It had told of the residents in the neighborhood complaining about the changes affecting the area. The Tommy Hilfinger clothing stores and Calvin Kline outlets moving in were the cause of several of the other businesses to begin to close. The one's that had served the neighborhood residents.

Rents, both for business and residential, were on the rise, skyrocketing in the surrounding neighborhood. The real estate craziness had apartment rents climbing to close to a thousand a month for a one-bedroom apartment.

It always amazed JB that how much a person paid for rent was considered a completely proper conversational topic in New York. Ask how much a guy you had just met at a party paid for their place and you had a thirty minute diatribe going for you.

◈ ◈ ◈

Len Matthews and JB had been friends with each other over the last several years. Both even lived in the same building on the Eastside of the city. That was a three story brownstone turned into separate apartments. JB, a successful mystery writer, was also part owner of the building they lived in. His place was on the first floor. Len had a studio on the second floor. As a popular actor he was familiar to those who attended the Broadway theater on a regular basis. He was also recognizable to most New Yorkers from numerous appearances in the gossip rags before he got sober in the past year. Not that that was a problem in the city. It was one of the things Len most appreciated about New York. The anonymity provided a reason for putting up with many of the inconveniences. That its citizens had a complete and utter disregard for most any celebrity was a huge selling point for living there. Your run-of-the-mill everyday celebrity could walk around town and be ignored just like everyone else.

That's why Len was startled to hear his name in a muffled call coming from somewhere there on the Avenue. They were standing just past a Greek diner and a deli at the corner of Seventy-second Street. To be precise, they were just walking in front of the awning roofed sidewalk cafe next door to the deli. Len, trying for cool, tried to ignore the interruption by the rude unknown fan. But the fan wasn't willing to take the hint. There soon was a loud banging on the window of the restaurant. From the inside.

Persistent little cuss, Len thought. Maybe the cretin would go away if Len simply continued to ignore him. But then, an actor's ego being what it was, he had to follow the noise. He looked over and saw a petite blond woman inside the cafe frantically waving her arm at him.

Len's hands went to his mouth. He went into a semi-squat while his face broke into a huge grin. And then his knees began to jerk. He resembled nothing less than a dodo bird on cocaine. JB watched bewildered as Len literally leaped to the window, and still hopping up and down, started slapping his palms on the glass.

"I'll be right in, Sweetie!" he yelled.

The lady inside nodded happily, then sat back in her table

Len, as far as JB could figure, was acting similar to a schoolgirl seeing her best friend on the schoolyard. Childlike. Not grown up behavior. In public, yet. But, that was Len. Outrageous behavior had become expected. A great deal of Len's charm was his enthusiastic take on life.

Len turned back to face JB.

"Oh, lighten up, JB. I see that disapproving look. Be glad I take some joy in what's going on around me. Don't you get it? I'm your own personal Auntie Mame, you sod." He wiped at an imaginary mark on his coat front. "That lady inside is Lee Arden. Do you know her?"

JB knew *of* her, but not her personally. She was a Broadway musical theater legend. And had been one for years and years. Probably more years than even Lee herself wanted to remember.

Lee Arden had been a white blond sprite who had started her Broadway career as a dancer back in the 1950's. That was when she eclipsed the leading lady with an Apache dance in her very first Broadway show. To the critic's delight. She then went on to star in a gaggle of successful musicals up until the Nineteen-seventies. She appeared most especially in musicals directed by her favorite dance director, partner, and soon after they met—husband. He was the equally famous choreographer and director, Teddy Brewster.

Teddy was a bright star in his own right. He was credited with having created a style of dance for Broadway that was his alone. With Lee Arden as his muse he had created movements and steps that put his dancer's feet and arms at odd and sometimes even awkward angles. Together, Lee Arden and Teddy Brewster had invented movements jerky and often unwieldy for their dancers to perform. The resulting numbers were always highly interesting and absolutely right for each show they appeared in. Dancers came to love the steps for their challenge. Audiences loved the shows they were performed in for their quirkiness and audacity. And, of course, all that style and panache they were renowned for came straight from Teddy Brewster, their creator. He had been called the Noel Coward of modern dance. A Cole Porter of hoofers. Plus he had been able to further imbue his work with a degree of substance far beyond the narrow lanes of Broadway. He'd ended up directing for both ballet and opera, won awards for film and television, hell, he'd even conquered radio. All during a varied and much fabled career. Then he'd been through a rough patch with two shows and a movie resounding failures. But, like many before him, now he was planning to make his return and a comeback on Broadway.

His latest venture was undertaken for exactly that reason. Comebacks would revitalize a career—ask Judy Garland—and Teddy's needed just that. To do it he had been directing the first full-scale revival of *Mrs. MacKenzie's Muddle* since its original run over twenty years before. The use of Teddy Brewster as director was at the behest of his long time collaborator and producer Ronald Prescott. However, according to the gossip rags, it had been a contentious and battle fueled rehearsal period. All the problems the show was having were reported dishingly by the likes of Liz Smith, Cindy Adams, Rex Reed, and their ilk in their daily or weekly newspaper columns.

Len ran back to JB. "I've got to go in and see them. She's a friend. Do you want to wait?"

"No, I'll come. It's starting to get cold."

And it was. New York was buckling down for the coming winter. You could feel it in the air. JB pulled his light weight jacket tighter around himself. It was a bit thin for this early on a Sunday morning, but, as a long time New York City resident he knew that by afternoon, after some sun began pouring down on the concrete streets, it would be perfect.

Len disappeared inside the cafe. JB followed him in, turned at the doorway and aimed out the arched opening onto the wooden platform that the seating area had managed to steal from the public sidewalks. It provided eight more tables for the restaurant, but left only a narrow path outside for pedestrians to walk on. Two people could get by each other, God forbid a third was along with them. He would have to hold back or be tipped off the curb.

Len was already seated at the table and gabbing excitedly with Miss Arden. Or Lee, as Len was calling her. Sitting next to her was the man himself, Teddy Brewster. He was, by then, Lee's ex-husband. There had been a short disastrous marriage between the two stars several years before. It lasted just about long enough to produce their son, Christopher. They had soon separated, but, at first, remained married. "For the time being" they said. They had issued a joint statement that explained bonds between people sometimes weakened over time. That "time" was a matter of mere months didn't seem to matter. They were adamant that there was no animosity between them. They would remain friends. Behind the stairs and at dinner tables all over the city it was asked if Teddy's numerous infidelities hadn't been the main component in their separation.

Six months after the statement they were divorced. Of course, that didn't make the slightest difference to their working relationship. No legal arrangement could keep them from still working together. Lee had, even before their marriage, been functioning as Teddy's assistant and partner. If truth be known, it had often been detrimental to her own career. She would refuse part after part to stay in the shadow of Teddy Brewster. There were plays by other producers that came along that she was tempted by, but Teddy would work his usual magic and keep Lee around playing only in his shows. Mostly, it became clear as time passed, because he needed her to continue managing his life.

As their unconventional arrangement continued, as Lee was drawn deeper and deeper into Teddy's magnetic field, Lee began to find new depths to her obsession. She allowed Teddy to become her full time job, her reason for living. She was his agent, his manager, his mother, his supplicant. Common knowledge had it that Lee Arden considered Teddy Brewster to be a singular genius. Of course, you also have to realize he was being considered the same by almost everybody on Broadway too. So Lee's obsession was reinforced by all that outside attention being heaped at Teddy's feet. Teddy Brewster was considered one of Broadway's chief innovative and celebrated dance creators of not just the last few years, but of the last century. Not since Isadora had shocked the dance world in the Nineteen-hundreds had there been such an artist.

Teddy Brewster was back then having his turn in the light, and had taken full advantage of it. Teddy was a force of nature in and of himself. A notorious womanizer, party-guy, and scalawag, he had, if you can imagine it, managed to scandalize even jaded New Yorkers during the swinging 60's with his shenanigans. And all the while he was still turning out hit after hit on the stage.

But as the Sixty's turned to the Seventy's and then the Eighty's he had floundered. A movie was a box-office failure, two shows, worked on for years in workshops and limited performances, were brought to Broadway and didn't play. Critics hated them. Audiences actually booed them. Teddy, it was being said, had lost his edge. The fabled career was over. And it was for several years. Oh, there were projects he worked on, but nothing would work out. Financing would fall apart or something else would go wrong. Years went by. Teddy Brewster was never forgotten but was definitely under the radar. A once-was.

Until earlier this year. Ronald Prescott, his friend and long time producer, had came to the rescue. He'd used his numerous financing and producing skills to mount a revival of the biggest hit of twenty years before. *Mrs. MacKenzie's Muddle*. It would be Teddy's comeback vehicle.

Lee Arden, stalwart that she was, had remained devoted to Teddy. She stayed with him, even when he hit the skids. Even when he continued to cheat on her with several of the female dancers in his company. What had made that more difficult was that most of these women were younger than Lee by twenty years or so. It was a double slap for her. Lee, unflinching as she was, had weathered the affairs like a proverbial trouper. She allowed Teddy his infidelities and still remained by his side. She stayed on as his muse, working as his assistant and the star of his productions. She continued to work with him every chance she could get. Love and devotion have been known to take odd turns occasionally. Lee Arden and Teddy Brewster, in their continuing close relationship, despite their rocky history, were a prime example.

Murder: Maybe?

Lee Arden, for her part, was a Broadway Baby in the purest sense of the appellation. A darling of the critics she had captured audiences in show after show with her seeming naiveté and charm. There was also an unrealized and underlying sex appeal about her. An eroticism even she didn't know she had. She was also considered by everyone to be one of the nicest women working in the theater. You couldn't find a single person who had a bad thing to say about her. On either coast. Not even the marriage to Teddy and its disastrous ending was fodder enough for the naysayers to abandon her, although the tabloids at the time had a field day. Splashed in foot high letters the papers had reported every nuance of the divorce and its aftermath.

Through it all she remained unscathed. She always maintained that Teddy Brewster was a living genius, with a capital G, but theirs was a *"Who can live with a Genius?"* sort of marriage. Then she would explain her reason for staying around the great man as her awe of his abilities. "If one is an artist themselves, as I hope I am, there is no way I will miss out on working with a genuine Genius. I mean, would you?"

That sentiment became her final answer to why she remained in Teddy's orbit long after their marriage was over. It was repeated often and soon became a part of the legend.

◆ ◆ ◆

Lee was now saying to Len, "So, we just got him out of the hospital and stopped here for brunch. You know how awful hospital food is?" She patted Teddy Brewster's arm. "He's much better, but he has to take it easy."

Teddy, looking annoyed, said, "You know I'm sitting right here."

He'd had, just three weeks before, his second heart attack. His first had only been a few months before that. This second attack came on while he was in the middle of a particularity acrimonious rehearsal with his show.

Those circumstances had made the headline the next day in the *Page Six* column of *The Post*. Then his condition was followed squib by quip for the next several days after. New Yorkers probably knew as much about Teddy Brewster's medical condition as his doctors. The gossip columns reported daily on Teddy's outrageous behavior while hospitalized. All night parties, gambling, booze, broads, nurse races, pill bingo. Teddy's antics had been deemed of inordinate interest to the readers of the local gossip columns. Even *People* magazine made mention, and the local New York papers, except for the *Times*, followed his and the show's problems in even greater detail. Fodder for the mill.

Mrs. MacKenzie's Muddle was a much-loved, if not overly sacchharine, musical, and Teddy, as the director of its revival, was said to be making some sweeping changes to the entire show. Putting his star, Betty Kane, into bizarre mechanization's and kinky scenes. Teddy was said to be making the sweet bucolic musical into an outright sex farce, with chorus girls as whores and actresses found starkers in the wrong people's beds. And there were more raunchy goings on being reported daily. The hubris of the rehearsals was what was causing such bitter fights between the principals and the producers. Teddy, in the midst of all this, then had his second attack. That led to an emergency bypass operation. Then, less than a week after that operation, Teddy had left the hospital.

Earlier that same morning. Go explain, but now here he was in a restaurant on Columbus Avenue at Sunday brunch with JB and Len.

❧ ❧ ❧

JB, standing beside the table that morning, did think Teddy looked pale and sort of "out of it". That's what the late morning papers had headlined it—*Teddy Out Of It*. Of course, they meant the hospital. JB felt it might have applied more to Teddy himself.

The paper had gone on to re-describe some of the weird behavior that had led to Teddy's attacks, his bypass, and now his recovery. Although, it did appear he wasn't exactly on the deathbed the newspapers had implied he was on. But JB had to think he didn't look all that chipper either. He looked like a sick man in need of a great deal of rest. Instead he was sitting in a public restaurant sucking on his always present cigarette. It dangled from his lip as usual. It was rumored that he even showered with one, although how he kept it lit raised a few questions.

You'd have thought that the doctors would have made him quit smoking, but the Teddy everyone knew wouldn't have listened if they had tried. He was a live his life to the fullest kind of guy. He was another follower of Mame Dennis' mantra that life was a banquet. Teddy, it seemed, was determined to make a pretty corpse. Booze, women, pills, and work were always and forever his main vices. And the people around him tended to excuse his outrageous excesses because he was just so damned talented. He would be forgiven any of his indulgences and peccadilloes.

Len introduced JB to Lee Arden and he was invited to sit. He grabbed a chair from another table and sat at the front, in the aisle, since there was another person taking up the remaining seat at the table for four already.

That person was sitting next to Len. Taking that seat was Lee and Teddy's son, Christopher Brewster. JB guessed he was meant to be there as support for his mother, as there had been some real animosity between Teddy and his son over the years. They had filled even more newspaper columns with their fights and arguments than Madonna's latest delinquent escapades ever could. Christopher and Teddy Brewster had a rocky and contentious relationship at the best of times. It was the result of what happens when two members of the same family are also competitors in the same business.

Rivalries developed between the two men that should have had no place in any parental relationship. However, when those monstrous show business egos come into play it can, and in the case of the Brewster duo, did happen. Much to his father's annoyance Christopher had been anointed an up and coming young prodigy of a theater director. With several regional and Off-Broadway plays to his credit before he even graduated college. It had added salt to an already festering wound. When it was reported he would debut on Broadway with his first play the next season Teddy and his son had actually exchanged blows. A fist fight at Elaine's one evening had been splashed all over the headlines. It was the worst blow their relationship could have taken.

Right then, in the restaurant, to JB the kid just looked sullen. And ticked-off. And incredibly sexy. JB was looking at a stunning young man of twenty-four, slouched lazily at the back of the table. The boy had inherited the best features of both his star parents. He was blond, muscular, and incredibility lithe. The man had the kind of movie star looks that made it hard for JB's jaw not to drop to his chest while his tongue rolled out across the table like some Tex Avery cartoon character.

There was much chitchat as everyone settled and introductions were made. Teddy, not interested, sat quietly and self-absorbed as the buzz went on around him. Then he coughed. That got Lee's attention. He started rubbing at his eyes. Lee asked if he was all right.

"I'm okay," he answered. "Just more tired than I thought." He wriggled inside his coat. Hunched, he said, "Can we go home?"

Lee, switching to caretaker mode, said, "Of course. You go wait outside and I'll take care of the bill." She bussed his cheek. "Wait for me."

Teddy got up and stood still for a moment, gathering his strength, then heaved a sigh, maybe hoping to grab enough air to push him forward. He sucked it in, then dragged his body toward the front door.

Lee raised her arm and signaled a waiter over. Christopher stood, excused himself, and started to follow his father. Lee was saying her good-byes to Len while she counted out the change for her bill.

There was a crash. It was a loud bang on the plate glass window right outside the door. Loud enough to cause the restaurant to quiet and turn their attention to the front of the establishment. A customer at the back even stood to see better what had happened. The sound had come from a man's body falling heavily against the tinted plexi-glass panel of the outer door. The man then lurched off the step, staggered along the sidewalk, and then slammed against the glass and slid down to the street. It was that noise that had warranted the attention of everyone inside. The news spread like a flame that a man had collapsed.

People outside were stopping and bending down to him, not necessarily from concern, but out of annoyance, because the narrow walkway wasn't built for bodies lying sideways blocking pedestrian traffic. A crowd was gathering.

Murder: Maybe?

Lee looked up at the noise going on outside and instantly stood at attention. Concern shadowed her expression. "It's Teddy," she said. "He's had another attack."

And she was gone.

Dance: Ten

TWO

◆◆◆◆◆◆◆◆◆◆◆◆◆◆◆◆Teddy
Brewster—Broadway Great~Broadway Legend—was dead.

JB could tell that by the time he and Len got outside
the restaurant onto Columbus Avenue. They had followed
behind Lee when she realized that Teddy was in trouble. JB
and Len got to the door and saw Christopher was kneeling
with a now crumpled Lee in his arms. Crying, her hand was
stretched out and rubbing at Teddy's chest. "Why? Why?"
she wailed.

JB turned to Len, "Give me your raincoat."

Len passed it over to JB in a daze. He had been talking
with this now dead man only minutes before. Death never
seemed so fast and fickle as right then. It was only a snap
of the fingers and gone.

JB knelt and covered the body with Len's coat. Teddy's
feet protruded from under it. Even in death they possessed
a danseurs elegance. They were posed as if he was doing a

step in one of his routines. Somehow a fitting tribute to the person he was. At least that's what the photographer from *The Post* flashed on when his picture was used on the front page of the next morning's paper.

When JB leaned beside Teddy to lay out the coat, his head snapped around. He'd noticed a whiff of something, a smell lingering in the air over Teddy's body.

Poppers?

It was poppers. He knew it was. JB was smelling amyl-nitrite. That's odd, he thought to himself. Poppers were a liquid that caused the heart to beat faster. Used by gay men in the disco's of the Nineteen-seventy's. At Studio 54, that sort of thing. And they were still used by many gay men for sex. Oh, yes, and for heart problems too. He shrugged. Maybe it wasn't so odd then?

JB spotted a nasal applicator still wrapped in Teddy's hand. The source of the smell he realized. It was one of those white plastic tubes that a person would stick in their nostrils to breathe in the menthol it was supposed to contain. To open nasal passages, as the magazine ads would have it. Available at your local pharmacy. JB wanted to check it out, and reached forward to take it. He stopped. Why do you want that?, he wondered. It's over the counter stuff. No big deal. Instead he left it for the forensic boys to find. They could figure out its significance.

He stood. "Maybe you should take your mother inside until the police get here, Christopher. Get her something to help calm her." Christopher nodded at JB's suggestion, stood, and began to guide Lee toward the front door.

Once they were out of earshot, Len stepped up beside JB. "That's an eighty dollar raincoat I'll never use again."

"Why, because it gave a dead man some dignity? And I happen to know it was a thirty dollar *London Fog* knockoff you bought on Orchard Street last winter."

"Even so, its gruesome. I'll have to get another coat."

"Fridays. Just before sundown. That's the best time to shop on the Lower East Side. Try to be the last sale of the day."

JB and Len were directing foot traffic on the sidewalk around the corpse of Teddy Brewster while they talked and waited for the cops to get there. They soon arrived and took over directing the foot traffic, which relieved JB and Len.

They went immediantly back inside to where Lee Arden and Christopher were sitting, if for no other reason than to comfort and commiserate with them. JB could see the next day's *Daily News* headline: *Broadway's Teddy Brewster Dies On Street He Loves*, purporting that Brewster was a full block over on Broadway. It made it a more show business kind of death that way. It would go down into the annals of theater history along with Gower Champion dying the day his show *42nd Street* opened.

Lee and Christopher were sitting at a table back in a corner surrounded by giant palms in bulbous ceramic containers. They, at the least, prevented prying eyes. Christopher had ordered hot tea and was trying to get Lee to drink some of it. She looked up at Len when he stood by their table.

"The foot patrol is here now, hon. But we still have to wait for the detectives. Isn't that right, JB?" Turning back to Lee, he finished, "JB writes mysteries. He knows about cops and these procedural things."

Lee, mostly to be polite JB suspected, said, "Is that right?" Then she looked up at him. "Oh. Wait, JB?" She brightened a tad. "Not Jeremy Bent? I read your book. The last one. Where you went back home. I mean the novel's character did."

It was a common misconception—that JB's mystery novels, which were often based on actual cases he had become involved in, were reporting and not the highly embellished and polished fiction they actually were. He would use made up versions of himself and his cohorts to star in the books. So readers often took them for truth, not the fictions he knew they were. It could get complicated.

"What's going to happen?" Lee now looked frightened as she asked her question.

"Once the homicide boys get here they'll ask a few questions then let you go home I imagine. It was natural causes, Ms. Arden. But there will have to be an autopsy since Teddy died on a public street."

"It was his heart. He hadn't recovered from his last attack. That was only three and a half weeks ago. Plus, he had the bypass operation. His heart couldn't survive another onslaught like that."

"Probably. But the forensic men will be able to establish exact cause of death."

Lee grabbed Christopher's hand. "I knew we should have gone straight home. He needed to rest. Gain back his strength."

"Mother. Stop. Teddy insisted. You know how he is? Or was. No, he had to stop by the rehearsals and schmoose with the cast and crew for an hour."

"He had a meeting this morning with the cast of his show? After just leaving the hospital?" Len sounded surprised.

Christopher answered. "There were concerns over the financing of the show since Teddy's attack."

"Still, that's a lot of people to have to work when your feeling good." Being social, even when well, but especially when ill, could be exhausting for anyone. "After his heart attack that must have been a real chore for him."

Len knew whereof he spoke. He had just returned to New York from a road show engagement of a musical. After appearing on several TV shows he was able to afford to go on the road with a play that he had hoped had a chance of coming to Broadway. It had closed in Philadelphia. Book problems were the announced reason. Len knew better. He had watched the infighting about money between the producers and the director even while they were all playing nice with the cast and crew.

Shows were costing huge amounts to finance these days. Which required multiples of producers, all with their own ideas of how the show should be run. Len's sojourn as Captain Hook in *Wendy and Hook* was in a show that had to be financed at close to a million dollars. With all the special effects and costume expenses it turned out it was too expensive to run at a profit. The show would have needed full houses every performance for three years to just break even. Closing had been inevitable. Len was guessing that Teddy had been having similar problems with his own show. Teddy's recent heart attack had probably set off alarms at insurance companies all over the East Coast. And, even if it jeopardized his health Len could see why Teddy would want to appear at a rehearsal as soon as he could. To quiet fears, to reassure the cast and crew. And the producers.

Teddy was working on *Mrs. MacKenzie's Muddle,* a musical hit from several years before. It was scheduled to star its original leading actress, the inimitable Betty Kane. She had originally starred as the meddling Mrs. MacKenzie in the mega musical twenty years before. The part had made her internationally famous. In fact, she had been playing the show all over the country and in Europe ever since. She was said to be willing to play it at grocery store openings if there was a stage and an orchestra supplied. It was her defining role.

But with Teddy's radical ideas about what he wanted to do with the show there was trouble brewing. He wasn't going to do a repeat of the original; he was directing a re-interpretation, with his signature style imposed on the old material. His ideas were newly re-creating the old musical melodrama.

For one thing he had wanted to replace Betty Kane in the lead with a younger woman. His choice was his lead dancer and current mistress. A real beauty named Jillian Morgan. Teddy wanted Betty to play the disapproving mother part instead. That hadn't set at all well with Miss Kane. She was notoriously proprietary about *Mrs. MacKenzie's Muddle.* She had the part down by rote. On that first day of rehearsal she carried with her a loose leaf binder. In it was her personally annotated script of the show. She handed it to Teddy and said, "That's my performance, bub. Do your stuff around it."

Teddy, when he opened it, found written down in Betty's flamboyant scrawl every movement, every voice intonation, every gesture of the part of Mrs. Mackenzie. Merman was famous for freezing a performance like *Bird's Eye.* Betty had her performance engraved in stone.

Which was an enormous problem for Teddy. He was demanding a looser, brighter concept of the character than Betty had ever provided. And, if he couldn't have a new Mrs. MacKenzie—Betty's contract prevented it—then he was determined to pull that new interpretation out of Betty herself.

It had been a fretful difficult rehearsal period and was thought to have been a huge contributor to the conditions that caused Teddy's heart attacks. Definitely the second attack. It could even be blamed for the open heart surgery that was performed soon after. And was the reason Teddy was so weak that last morning with JB and Len. All of this was public knowledge since it had been reported and scuttle-butted up and down Broadway for all to hear over the last few weeks.

Lee, sitting in that cafe, her world shattered, her dance master dead, was at that moment white-faced and suffering from shock. Still, she was able to explain to them his reason for the meeting that morning. "Teddy wanted to prove to the producers that he was well enough to go on directing the show. There were rumors about replacing him. He wanted to calm them. He even called his next rehearsal for tomorrow at noon." She began to cry again.

Len mused, "That means they'll have to find a new director." JB waved him quiet.

He shrugged and mouthed, "What?"

Christopher looked up. "No, they won't. I can take over the show. Teddy and I discussed his ideas while he was in the hospital. We spent a lot of time together while he was sick. We ended up talking shop. Director to director. It really brought us closer together. I think I know what Teddy would have wanted."

Lee took Christopher's arm. "Do you think the producers will hire you? It would be a Godsend. Teddy believed in this show. I've invested in it myself."

"Then I'll have to do it. To protect your investment, Mother."

◆ ◆ ◆

And that bit of news—the son taking over the father's production—was announced at the end of Teddy's obituary the next day. The obit that was a page one headline in *all* the New York papers, including the *Times*. They carried the notice below the fold on the front page. Reporters loved the angle that Christopher would now take over the show. It provided a satisfactory finish to their stories. It was the kind of theatrical moment Broadway tales are knitted from. Assuming the son made a hit of it. That he wouldn't produce a bomb.

Three

◈◈◈◈◈◈◈◈◈◈◈◈◈◈◈T he
next morning JB was coming back from buying the paper
when he ran into Len in the lobby of their building. "Where
are you off to? Aren't you usually in bed until noon every
day?"

"Not today. I'm going over to Lee Arden's. There's a
wake for Teddy at her place. And since we were there when
it happened." He shrugged. "I kinda feel like I should go."

"Humm. Can I tag along? I have a couple of questions
I want to ask."

Len sniffed. "You know, sometimes I'm sorry you ever
started this mystery writing thing of yours. It's made you
awfully suspicious. For you there's something sinister in
everything that happens. What could you possibly want to
ask about?"

"I don't know about sinister. Fretful might be a
better word. What I'm wondering about is that popper

smell. That's one thing. You noticed it too, didn't you?" Len nodded. "Why would a man with a weak heart want to use something that would cause his heart to beat more rapidly? That's something I wonder about."

"A reasonable question, I suppose. Anything else, Miss Marple?"

"Who would have wanted Teddy dead?"

"Come on, you're not suggesting it was a murder? But how? We were there. Nobody was near Teddy when he died."

"I direct you back to the poppers. If his heart was as weak as was reported and then started beating too fast it would kill a person, right? So, who would give Teddy Brewster poppers?"

"You've really been worrying this, haven't you?"

"Kept me awake most of the night."

"Well, for God's sake, don't let on to Lee that you suspect anything remotely like this. She's devastated enough by his death."

"Does that mean I can come with you?"

"Sure. But, be gentle. Okay?"

The cab dropped JB and Len off in front of Lee Arden's West 60's building. They walked up the stoop, through the glass outer doors and into a tiny foyer. A table and mirror were against one wall. A place for mail and flyers. Against the other wall was the apartment's intercom system. There were only two units in the building. Bottom floor and upper. According to the brass nameplate Lee had the upper. Len rang and they were buzzed inside to the elevator. They rode it to the second floor where the doors opened onto a short landing and another door. This one was draped with a huge black ribbon. Len rang at that door and mumbled, "A bit Victorian don't you think?" eyeing the silk bow.

"Well, Lee is from Ohio. Or is it Nebraska? One of the Plains states. They can be sort of old world out there."

"Are you kidding? Nowadays? With television those people out there can be trendier than here in Manhattan. They do tend to a more Vegas-ie look though. There's not a lot of Anne Kline wandering around. Betsy Johnson would be ripped off your back..." The door opened, which stopped

Len from finishing his thought.

At the door was a brittle thin young woman who looked like one of the older dancers from the Ballinchine Studios over at City Ballet. You would often see the students in their tights and leotards running to make their classes at Lincoln Center, just a few blocks away. The pulled back topknot hair style they called a bun-head was so tight on this girl it gave her a kind of rictus smile.

They were ushered onto a narrow ledge supported by a black iron railed stairway. Lee had both floors of the building after all. You looked down from the ledge onto a living room done all in white. Soaring ceiling high framed windows at the far end provided a view of trees and the back gardens of neighboring apartments. Rugs, tables, couches, chairs, pillows, even the picture frames set about on tables, were covered or painted in varying degrees and shades of white. The snowstorm effect from all that non-color, along with the silver metal hanging grid of overhead lights, made the black cloth covered wall mirrors stand out like cruel slashes on a snowy hill.

Down in the center of the lower floor Len spotted Lee. She was sitting in a slip covered chair and a half. Her arm was leaning on the wide rest with her feet pulled up comfortably under her. She wore her standard costume, which was a leotard top and dance tights. A sweater was slouched over her shoulders with the sleeves tied at the neck. Knitted leg warmers pooled at her ankles and she wore a pair of *Capazio* dance heels. They were all in black befitting the occasion. It made her stand out starkly against the paleness of the background.

There was a group of people sitting on the floor around her chair, listening to Lee tell the story of how she and Teddy met.

"We were both cast in our first off-Broadway shows then. That's where we met. At that first rehearsal. Teddy had vastly more experience than I did. I was just out of Madam Celeste's Dance School in Chillicothe and Teddy had already been in nightclubs and movies out in Hollywood. But we got picked to be partners in the second act finale. We did a lovers quadrille for seven shows a week. How could I not fall for him?" She dabbed at her eye with a tissue she held, then continued. "We got engaged soon after Teddy choreographed his first show. That was *Blondie*. I was in that with him. I had a featured part. Right after we'd done *Cleo: 5 to 7* was when we got married. I had the lead in that show. It was based on a French film from the sixty's. About a girl waiting for the results of a medical test. If it was a negative diagnosis it meant she was going to die. I know it sounds so morbid, but it was a fun sprightly show about the joys of living. I loved doing Teddy's steps. He had created the dances just for me. He even wrote the book for *Cleo* himself, adapting the screenplay for the stage. It was tailored just for me, for the sort of dancer I am. We got married the day after the opening. I remember because Christopher was born exactly nine months later." That got a chuckle from her appreciative audience.

Len, now standing with JB near Lee's chair, also remembered that the show contained six of the best songs ever written for a Broadway musical. It had a score that was right up there alongside *Gypsy* for its brilliance. And it had that then stunningly new choreography in Teddy's knock-kneed eccentric style, danced by what was soon called the most limber woman in show-business: Lee Arden. *Cleo: 5 to 7*, based on a French movie of the same name, ran for one thousand and twenty-five performances before it closed. Lee was the principal dancer in all six of the numbers during the show. Six dance numbers in two hours and thirty-seven minutes. And she never missed a performance. Not even when she started showing her pregnancy with Christopher. They simply redesigned the costumes and she kept on going. She even had the baby on a Monday when the show was dark. A trouper with a vengeance. *Cleo: 5 to 7* made Lee Arden a star. For his part, Teddy Brewster, with Lee as his wife and muse, went on to create another four hit musicals for her; until she finally retired in nineteen-seventy-eight. She'd been retired from dancing since then, although she did venture out to Hollywood for movies and occasional TV guest roles.

Teddy had stayed in New York for most of his career. Directing and producing for the theater. This latest show Teddy had been working on was to be his tenth to bring to Broadway.

The group at Lee's feet asked another question and she was off on another story. JB, still standing next to Len, had heard this one on her last Letterman appearance, so he looked around the gathering. After the rows of floorsitters at Lee's feet there was a medium sized crowd of standees conversing with each other in lowered voices, with occasional bursts of louder laughter. To them it was a cocktail party; not the something more serious it actually was. Of course, from what JB could see, Lee might have thought so too. She was definitely on stage, playing the raconteur for her admiring crowd. Show biz people, ya know?

JB turned toward the area beyond the arch on the right. In there, where normally there was a formal dining room, was now a draped table set with food, a bar to the left. Both had waiters standing behind them. "Good God!" he whispered to Len, "She's catered the funeral."

"What did to you expect?" Len shot back. He was taking a plastic plate, a couple of hor d'oeuvres, and a napkin from the tray of a passing waiter. "The biggest star on Broadway out roaming the crowd in an apron serving Apple Pan Dowdy to the mourners? This is New York. What else would she do to feed all these people?"

JB, also taking some food, said, "I just meant that this feels the same as a cocktail party in here. The atmosphere is so festive. Is Lee going to do songs at the piano?"

"You should know the answer to that one, JB? It's show business. Over the top? Which Cole Porter rightly said?"

"Like you tend to be so often, huh? And that was *You're The Top*. And it was one of his gayest songs ever. Now, come on, we should both go pay our respects to the widow."

They took their plates of canapés—those odd little combinations of foods on crackers that New York caterers seem to favor. Chutney and rutabaga together anyone? — and worked their way toward the chair Lee was ensconced in. She sat there looking every inch the forlorn waif she was advertised as. Actually, still looking—at well into her fifties—the gamin—young and sweet, with a dash of flirty. Len went up to her at the end of her story and leaned over. "So sorry, Lee."

"We're going to spread Teddy's ashes out at our place in

Southampton. Teddy always loved it out there." She dabbed again at her eye. Len wanted to believe it was for real, but he had spent too many years around too many actresses to always believe an emotion when he saw one. In Lee's case it probably was on the up and up. She was known to be a devoted worshipper at the altar of Teddy Brewster. His death, for her, was a definite blow.

JB stepped up then and bent to say something similar to what Len had. Then Lee kept hold of his hand and he felt he had to continue the conversation. He needed to say more. But what? He had noticed while waiting to talk with her what looked like hundreds of framed pictures of Teddy standing all over the room. There were frames lined on ledges, along shelves and on tables. From various stages of his career, they were dominated by a giant painted portrait of him hanging over the fireplace. Like the mirrors, it was draped with black silk, yards of it, from corner to corner across the top, streaming down the sides to the mantle. It made the painting look like Teddy was stepping on stage at one of the strip joints where he had started out as a tap dancer between the naked lady acts. The painting had Teddy holding a tambourine while striking a jaunty pose. It was a prop that Teddy would find a way to inject into every one of his shows. It was for him like a top hat for Fred Astaire, or a derby for Bob Fosse.

Still bending to Lee, JB said, "Love the decor. But isn't rococo shrine hard to keep clean?"

Without turning a bleached white hair, Lee replied, "Oh, I have Esmarelda in to help every week. She's a saint. A real angel."

"I guess that's exactly what you would need for the job now, isn't it? An angel?"

Thinking that might be enough said, JB backed away. Holding his plate chest high he went out amongst the standees, leaving Lee to tell more of her Teddy stories.

Standing by the bookcase he found Christopher Brewster, holding a similar plate to JB's at his own chest.

"Ever feel like a flamingo?"

"Or a Florida lawn ornament."

They laughed. Then stopped abruptly. Then looked at the floor for a moment.

"Uh, a nice gathering for your father, Christopher."

"Most of them are from his current show. They all want to know what's going to happen to their careers now that Teddy's dead. But, I'm going to fool them, JB. I can make *Mrs. MacKenzie's Muddle* a hit."

"Wasn't the project rocky to begin with? There were rumors that Teddy's concept for the show was pretty out there."

"You know what he was going to do? Dance it. The entire show was going to be choreographed. Do you see that girl over there. The one taking a sip of her drink? She was Teddy's lead dancer. He was going to have her play Mrs. MacKenzie as a young widow. With an equivalent young cast, requiring all new people. That was what was bothering everybody. The Mrs. MacKenzie part has traditionally been for a women of a certain age."

JB nodded. Parts for women of that age—too old for ingénues, to young for dowagers—were hard to find. Good parts for women over fifty were few and far between. Sure there was Angela Lansbury as Mame, Ethel Merman as Mama Rose. Carol Channing as Dolly. But that was about it. Maybe Mrs. Hannigan in *Annie* would qualify?

Christopher continued. "And I'm not going to buck that trend, JB. I intend to keep the part played by an older woman. But I am keeping most of the choreography Teddy did intact. What would you think of Lee Arden as Mrs. MacKenzie? With Betty Kane as her sister instead of her mother?"

"The two of them on stage together? That's a great idea. Can you get Lee to come out of retirement?"

"She hasn't really been gone. She was always working with Teddy on his routines. And she's only fifty-two. Not seventy-eight."

"No, but Betty's getting pretty close. And she's not a dancer."

"You know the answer to that? She on stage, and she's ageless. It's Mary Martin at close to forty playing a twenty-three year old Nellie Forbush. Betty can pull off being Mother's older sister. And she can do a soft-shoe with the best of them."

"Well, it would make a hell of a pairing. Will Betty

go along with it?"

"I need to get the job directing first. Then I can talk to her about casting and her role in the show."

"You mean they haven't offered it to you yet?"

"This afternoon, I suspect. There's a meeting of the shareholders. Here. In our dining room right over there, as a matter of fact. At four. Since Mom is one of the investors it made sense to have it here."

JB had to admit to himself that he was interested in the mechanization's of the Broadway theater. As least as a person who had a play produced on Broadway, as a member of the community, and, of course, as a gay man he was interested. No question about it. Such information provided built in dinner conversation all over New York. Broadway Musical was like a second language for many gay men in and around the city. Besides, if he didn't make sure to pass such knowledge he might gather on to Len—as possible auditions for him—then JB would have hell to pay. Even if it was one of those stereotypical thing's people said about gay people JB remained interested in the Broadway stage. Also, there were those niggling little questions he had about Teddy's death running around in his feverish grey cells, as Agatha Christie would call them. He decided to try to steer the conversation so he could ask Christopher about his suspicions without seeming snoopy or intrusive.

"Well, good luck." JB started to move backward. "I know you'll get the job. Once again, I'm sorry about your father." He turned and started to walk away. Then he pulled a *Columbo* and turned back. "You know, Christopher, I was wondering? Yesterday. When I put the coat over Teddy?"

"And thank you for that," Christopher said.

"What anyone would do. What I wondered was why Teddy had an inhaler in his hand. What was that for?"

"Oh, he had terrible sinus problems. You must have seen his menthol inhaler. He used it to open up the nasal passages. He carried it all the time."

"Is it possible there was something else in it?" JB hadn't smelled menthol. What he had smelled was definitely out of the nitrite family.

Christopher looked surprised, then said, "No, just menthol."

"Well thanks, Christopher. I hope we run into each other again. For coffee or something?"

"Sure."

JB was sure that wouldn't happen. Even if Christopher was a gorgeous young man and JB was, for lack of a better term, in thrall with him. He had actually considered grabbing the boy by the hair and dragging him out of his mother's apartment, through Central Park, and into his own cave over on the Eastside, where he would have had his way with him. Straight or not—and Christopher's sexual preferences hadn't been announced as of yet. He could have been straight. He could have been gay. Who knew? Probably not even Christopher. But Christopher Brewster was surely a hunk and a half. A twelve on a scale of one to ten. But he was also young. Twenty-four to JB's forty-one. Seventeen years.

JB had been here before. In this situation that is. An age difference was always sticky. Unfortunately, this sort of thing was happening to JB more and more of late. Getting someone age appropriate was becoming a real problem. Getting older in gay life sucked.

JB found Len talking with one of the male dancers from *Mrs. MacKenzie's Muddle.* A thinly muscled man who still managed youthful even though he hovered uncertainly somewhere in his late thirties. Handsome, it was obvious he had parlayed his good looks to win a place in the business. A leading man who hadn't quite made the grade and had settled for the chorus.

"Well, nobody knows what's going to happen?" he was saying. "And its too late in the season to get another show. What's an at liberty gypsy gonna do? If this show doesn't stay in rehearsal I may have to go back to my job at Mrs. Pepperdines."

That was a restaurant that served huge fruit filled muffins to ladies with tired feet in the vicinity of Bloomingdales.

"God, I hope not," Len commiserated.

"But you should have seen the way the show was going. Teddy was putting all kinds of wacky things into the thing, A sex ballet for Mrs. Mac and her lover, Mr. VanRoddy." He snorted. "Can you imagine? Geriatric genuflecting. Ugh. There was also this vaudeville parody he was working on.

Dance: Ten

And an awful dance that was nothing more than Teddy's musings on death. In a musical comedy? It was all so puzzling. And the producers were scared shitless. Poor Ronald."

"Ronald? You mean Ronald Prescott?" Len asked,

The dancer looked over the room. "He's over there," he pointed. "The one that has the permanent sweat filled forehead. In the Saville Row suit?"

Len and JB both looked. He was sitting on the ledge of the fireplace looking up at the underbosoms of one of the women dancers. Her leotard top was accenting her assets and he was obviously interested in handling her fiduciary funds.

"She's causing him to sweat, right?" Len said.

"Or is it the real possibility that the show will close and take with it the entire investment Ronald raised," the dancer said. "A million plus expenses ain't chump change, you know? If the show did tank Ronald would have to pay it all back to his investors."

A little while later, when JB had wandered off again, he found himself talking with Ronald himself. The producer wasn't the least bit shy about explaining his predicament.

"It's a huge gamble to go with a revival of an American musical. Which is what Teddy and I had decided to do. We were risking the wrath and the scorn of all the critics. They loved the original so much." Ronald shuttered, then looked hopeful. "But that's what revivals are for? Right? To re-think the root material. To re-invent it and show it in a new and exciting way. Look at the way they keep changing *Show Boat* every time they bring it back." It sounded to JB like a quotation from one of Teddy's pep talks at one or another of their producer's meetings.

Ronald shook his head. "I should have done what all the other producers are doing. Gone to London and bought the rights to a show there. Already proven. It's a guaranteed hit. You make back your investment right away. I had a chance to invest in *Cat's*. But did I?"

JB moved on. He was thinking it might be interesting to talk with the mistress. The one who Teddy had been planning to star in the show. How did she feel about all this?

Murder: Maybe?

Jillian was her name. Jillian Morgan. She was a dark haired natural beauty about twenty years Teddy's junior. She was full and curvaceous, which was the way Teddy liked his woman. No Ballanchine skinny sticks for him. Teddy loved the voluptuous. He favored women with a balcony you could do Shakespeare off of.

JB found her, extended his sympathies, and then mentioned to her how hard it must be, standing in the same room with Teddy's ex-wife.

"Please," she scoffed. "You want to know the truth? We're the best of friends. I know its weird, but Lee Arden is one terrific lady. She's asked me to work with her on a memorial of Teddy's work. A dance recital featuring his best routines from all of his shows."

"But what about your lead in *Mrs. MacKenzie's Muddle*? That was your chance to become a star. And it was taken away. Out from under you. Like a rug."

"Yeah, the stinker had to go and die on me? Couldn't have waited another couple of months? Until the show could open." She dabbed at her eye with a wad of tissue. "It was my chance, for Christ sake. Don't get me wrong. I'll miss him. But his timing was awful."

JB heard a ruckus at the front door and looked up.

Betty Kane had arrived. There was a confused magilla at the top of the stairs as coats were taken, and then Betty made her way down. She didn't walk down the stairs like normal people would do. She descended them. With her it was as if she was Dolly entering the Harmonia Gardens. There should have been a boy chorus with outstretched arms at the bottom of the staircase to do her justice. Betty entered every room the same way. As if it was an entrance in the play that her life was. Theatrical was a word invented for women like Betty Kane. Betty worked at looking the part too. Her face was so tight from her most recent plastic surgery that she looked exactly like the Hirshfield caricature that hung at Sardi's. JB wondered if he should look for the NINA's in her hair. The hair was bleached and coifed into a stiff bubble. Her clothes were the best Bergdorf's could offer and cut to fit like Mrs. Windsor's jewels. Exquisitely.

Behind her followed the current mate, Roger. He was

the star's husband, if such a job category exists. It was his task to allow Betty to play Lady Nicely while taking on the burden of making sure every little detail of her life was as she demanded it. And demand it she did. He was a secretary-slash-major-domo—with privileges. When she met him he was a second sting comedian in a Chicago standup room. Betty took a fancy to him. He was husband number six.

At the bottom of the stairs Betty held out her arms and started toward Lee, her fur stole dragging behind her. The room opened for her like the Red Sea in biblical stories. "Darling," she crooned. "I just got the news. We were out at the Hamptons, closing up the summer house, and I heard about it. So we just rushed back to be with you. The traffic was awful. Are there drinks? I'm dying for a Harvey Wallbanger."

Roger skittered off to find one for her. "Well," Betty said, as she stroked the fur of her mink. The hair smoothed under her hand. "I hope this terrible event will put some sense into Ronald's conker and he'll go back to the original script of *Mrs. MacKenzie's Muddle*. Teddy's ideas were just so outlandish, darling"

Lee smiled. "We'll discuss all that this afternoon, dear. You'll be at the meeting, right? There's a chance Christopher might take over. He has some ideas of his own."

Betty's eyes narrowed. "Such as?"

"You'll find out when we meet, dear. Meanwhile, here's your drink. Thank you Roger."

He stepped up and handed the drink to Betty. She grabbed it and sipped at the straw. "An inexperienced director? I don't know..."

Lee interrupted her. "Betty. Not now. At the meeting. Please."

Betty, with Roger tagging along behind in servile mouse position, went off to a corner to worry this new development. How would it affect Betty? That was all she was interested in. That was all her ego would allow her to be concerned about. Any event that happened, should it be personal—or for that matter, even an accident on the Long Island Expressway—was scrutinized for what consequences or benefits it might have for Betty Kane.

Totally self involved.

JB and Len came together again. "Do you want to stay?" Len asked.

"Not unless you do."

"Actually, I'm feeling a bit peckish. These hors d'oeuvres are not making it. How about brunch? Over at Company's?"

"Sounds good. Can we get a table? It's the brunch crowd you know?"

"Remember who your with, child."

Dance: Ten

Four

◆◆◆◆◆◆◆◆◆◆◆◆◆◆◆◆◆◆◆◆A
cab took them through the park and over to Third Avenue
where the restaurant was located. Brunch at Company's
was a popular meeting place for the Eastside neighborhood
gays. It was noisily crowded with a full bar of waiting
patrons when they stepped in.

Len's celebrity—what restaurant wouldn't want their
clientele to know a famous Broadway actor was there
with them? Although, JB mulled to himself, within the
gay and theatrical community, notorious probably was
a better description for Len. Before he got sober he was
the epicenter of several well-documented escapades. The
tabloids had loved him.

Len's celebrity got them a table ahead of someone else. JB
thought it was an abuse of Len's prominence, but he didn't
turn down the seating either. Once seated at a spectacularly
visible table and with a complimentary Mimosa in front

of JB, a virgin version in front of Len, they re-hashed the morning.

"JB, did you find out what you wanted?"

"Just picking at the lint balls on the sleeve of a proverbial sweater is all. I spend my nights creating murder plots for my books. Now I find myself looking for a plot in every situation I encounter. Is that healthy? I really should talk about it with my shrink."

"It is my firm belief that a shrink should only get rid of any neuroses that doesn't make the patient tons of money. Hate Mommy? So cliché. Murder plots? Is that neurotic? Maybe? But with medication nicely under control. And in your case quite profitable." Len opened his menu. "So what do you feel like?"

"I'm still wondering why anyone we met today would want Teddy dead? Who would benefit from his death? That's the first question I usually ask."

"How about the Eggs Benedict?"

"When the autopsy report is done I'll have a better sense of what I'm looking for."

"You're going to autopsy the eggs? Whatever for?"

"Huh? What are you going on about? We're having the Benedict, right? And another Mimosa." JB held up his glass. "So what are your plans for the day."

"Oh, I was going to do some cleaning this afternoon, but that has, thankfully, been changed. Now I have a meeting."

"A meeting."

"With Christopher and Lee and the producers."

"What for?"

Len leaned in with a sly smile on his face. "I was hoping you would ask." Then in a conspiratorial sounding tone, he said, "Christopher mentioned to me that Lee might make her comeback to Broadway with *Mrs. MacKenzie's Muddle*."

"He said the same thing to me."

Len leaned back. "Do you know its been almost ten years since Lee Arden was on the boards. Shameful. If they do get Lee to come back, then the director—who would be Christopher—would have to recast the show. He would need a younger man for the part of Mr. VanRoddy. Jerry

Rosen, who had the part with Betty as the star, is far to old to be Lee's partner. It would look vaguely incestuous between those two." He paused and then announced, "I'm being considered for the roll."

"Len, that's terrific."

Len couldn't contain his excitmeent any longer. "JB, its a leading man role. The straight romantic interest in a Broadway play that could be the biggest showcase of the last five seasons? And the next five seasons as well. This is simply huge. I'm supposed to meet with them at four this afternoon. So what I intend to do is go back to my place and rehearse." He taped two fingers at his throat. "To loosen up the pipes."

"Well, I have something more fun in mind for today. I'm going with my friend Charles to an exhibit of Lautrec posters at the Illustrators Society Gallery over on Lexington."

"And what's that all about? You and this Charles?"

Charles was a new friend for JB. Emphasis on friend. Charles had been a chance meeting one afternoon at the gay bar around the corner from JB's apartment a couple of months before. It had been hot then, at the end of summer, and the writing from the night before had gone lousy. A cold beer sounded just the remedy. Charles—who was also seated at the bar that afternoon—and JB got to talking. When Charles mentioned this club he belonged to—*The NY Jacks*—it had intrigued JB. A gay men's masturbatory club had sounded downright titillating. He got himself invited to a meeting being held that same night.

That meeting was held in another gay bar, *The Candle II*, over on the Westside of Manhattan—on Amsterdam Avenue, right off of Broadway. The club had taken over the whole place for the night. Charles, as a member, was JB's entry in. JB paid his entrance fee, got a wire basket and disrobed, ending up in his T-shirt, jockey shorts, and his cap. Loafers without socks finished off the costume for that night.

He found he was quickly enjoying himself and fit in with those who were re-living fantasies of circle jerks in the locker rooms of almost every high school gym in the country. It was a voyeurs dream evening come alive. While other men attending were poster boys for more esoteric gay male imaginings.

The bar was decorated in an urban version of cowboy style with pine boards, hay bales, and strings of coiled barbed wire running along the ceiling. There was a loft space built over the bar, with a stairway leading up at the side. There was another stairway to the downstairs basement area in the center of the room. That was surrounded by a railing that as the evening progressed became the main posing area for the men attending. Pretty men waiting to be admired. Similar to what went on in Victorian theater lobbies in the nineteenth century. And in the Elizabethan ages for thet matter. And probably even the Greek ages. Socrates had to find his boys somewhere.

The room was filled with men in all shapes and sizes. Butches and Metros. Young twinks to late 40's. All of them in tantalizingly varied degrees of nakedness. Jockstraps were much in evidence, along with derrick hats, leather vests, tank tops, and workman boots. Mirrored sunglasses were also popular. Bare ass was everywhere.

To fully explain *The NY Jacks* should probably be a bit more delicate. Instead. Here it is. Put bluntly. *The Jacks* was a quickly growing New York City social club for gay men to gather and masturbate. Jack off. Themselves and others. Hence the name. Open to all of those who might enjoy watching or participating in this activity with other men who were similarly minded. Basically, it was a safe-sex orgy. It was, to a great degree, a reaction to the AIDS crisis and the supposition that the disease could be passed by a single unsafe sexual contact. Gay men, in the early stages of the disease, had been reluctant to give up the sexual freedom they had achieved before AIDS had appeared on the scene. *The Jacks* were a safe-sex alternative to the orgy scene that had been around before. Having your cake and still licking the frosting, so to speak.

AIDS had slammed the New York gayworld like a damp washcloth only five years earlier. It had snapped at all of their behinds as many—so many—men had died from the raging disease in those early days. It put a damper on all gay sex for a time. What many gay men sorely missed was the freedom to have their sex whenever and with whomever they desired. They wanted it the same as the pioneers had created the sexual revolution back in the more promiscuous nineteen-seventy's. Orgies, backrooms, the docks, the trucks, video stores. All of them were open and available and hot back then. These places had lost any appeal when it was realized that HIV was sexually transmitted.

By late nineteen-eighty-six the gay community had been made fully aware of what sexual activities were safe and what were unsafe. It was also assumed by many that a single unsafe contact could infect you with the disease. *The Jacks* was a way to keep experiencing that seventy's backroom orgy mentality in a much safer environment.

A few years before, when less was known, a normal reaction to AIDS for many gay men was to crawl into a cocoon and give up sex totally. That might have lasted a weekend or two. Another solution was to fall back on the first and most prevalent sexual activity of them all. Five fingered, hairy palmed, slap the monkey, hand jobs. Wrap that up in locker room fantasies from high school and it made the whole *Jacks* scene attractive as an alternative to sex that might exchange fluids. When you also factored in that JB was a man who tended to observe what went on around him—necessary to his profession—then you had a situation made in heaven for him. He believed observation was requisite to his writing. But, to be frank, he was a voyeur at the core.

That voyeurism in equal proportion to the exhibitionists that had flocked to *The Jacks* meetings was a deciding component to his continued attendance. JB became a regular member after that first night.

▧ ▧ ▧

JB and Charles had planned, after the poster exhibit, on going to dinner. Then they would attend an evening with *The Jacks*. That part of JB's plans was information that Len didn't need to have.

There were parts of JB's life that Len wasn't made privy too. And vice-versa. It was mutually understood. Even with their history—they had been lovers for a couple of years in the early eighty's. Then had remained best friends after the breakup—Even with that history between them their lives were not open books to each other. They each had some areas that neither was invited into.

JB interrupted his musings to answer Len's question. "What;s going on with Charles? Nothing. I'm just doing something tonight with him? And don't get all giddy, Len. There's nothing there. Charles is only a friend."

"Friend, huh? This is the third or fourth weekend you've spent with him. What are you two up to?"

"None of your business, Mr. Snoopypants. I don't have to tell you everything I do."

Len sat back. It wasn't like JB to hold out on him. They shared almost everything, didn't they? Well, no, not every thing. Len hadn't mentioned to JB the dinner engagement he had for that evening, now had he? No real reason to, Len rationalized. It was simply a first meeting, anyway. It probably wouldn't amount to a hill of innuendo. Not even worth a mention. "I suppose not. But when you sink to schoolyard name calling I begin to think the worst. What the hell are you hiding?"

"I have nothing to hide. I am not a crook, as Richard Nixon once prevaricated. So let it go, all right?" To redirect the conversation JB then asked, "So Lee Arden will be coming back to Broadway?"

"Yes. Isn't that exciting? Although, I think there's a degree of desperation in the return."

"Why?"

"Well, she's heavily invested in the show, you know? Ronald Prescott couldn't get it completely financed from his own pool of investors, so she stepped in to help. Not surprising, really. You know how devoted she was to Teddy. I get the feeling that if the show doesn't play she will be broke-ola." He snapped a breadstick. "Plus, it could go a long way toward jump starting Christopher's career."

"Not to say bringing hers back to life too."

"True."

Christopher's own career had stalled over the last two years. He had started his career young. With his parents backing him he had little choice but to go into the family business. The business of show. He started directing his first plays as a teenager, working in several Off-Off Broadway productions located in tiny theaters scattered here and there over the New York theatrical landscape.

Those early productions, after high school graduation

and while on breaks from college, had led Christopher to being hired for gigs in Regional Theater, taking him to the outskirts of the arts on the great plains of America. While there he was able to mine a deeply held talent, perhaps inherited, perhaps simply a part of his genetic makeup. Wherever it came from he soon became an original voice and interpreter of the Midwestern angst. The works he guided were well reviewed and then, through some discreet finagling by a parent, had New York itself looking at him. Once returned to the city, he had directed two serious dramas to Off-Broadway success. Both had received raves from the critics and should have led to more.

But, it had stopped there. The next step should have been for Christopher to work on Broadway itself. That chance had never happened. It had been blamed mostly on economics. The cost of any straight play, especially with union rules—for instance, even a one character play was required to have a set number of musicians on staff—made them unprofitable. Audiences weren't interested. The right play hadn't been available. For whatever reason, Christopher hadn't worked in the theater for the past two seasons. There had been rumors of a play for the next fall, but nothing substantial enough to formally announce. That meant, for Christopher, this chance to take over his father's production of *Mrs. MacKenzie's Muddle* could make him and his career. If he brought in a hit he could write his own ticket from then on. JB wondered if that would be enough for the young man to commit a murder? Patricide? Was it worth a career that could be bigger than his father's? That could be a mighty strong motive. Murders had been done for less.

And what about Lee Arden? How would she benefit from Teddy's death? With this rumored return to the boards she would be reinventing her own career, and doing it in a star turn. She could be the toast-of-the-town for one more time. And she would be helping to make her son a star. Mother love? Ego rampant? Most likely a mix, JB would guess. Plus he also realized Lee stood to make a ton of money from the show. That is if it was produced and became a hit. She was a heavy investor in the thing. It would certainly be to her benefit for the show to go on.

Also, if Teddy was pushing the boundaries, as was rumored, would the show have been a hit? That was chancy at best. Even JB with his little bit of savey about the theater knew a bomb in the making when it was talked about the way Teddy's show was before his death. Unfortunately, Teddy, even before his first heart attack, had pissed off several critics with his remarks in print about them and their abilities to recognize art when they saw it. Teddy's art at least. They would have surely been out to get him for the remarks and might have negatively reviewed the show regardless of its quality. That wouldn't have set well with the producers, now would it?

Then again, JB decided, it was way out of character for Lee. Lee Arden had been Teddy's soulmate for nearly forty years. She had even subjugated her own career to the desires and wishes of this single man. She wouldn't turn on him now? Would she? Would Lee Arden, the woman that had remained, year after year, with Teddy as his muse and friend. His slave and serf. Entwined and bonded with him. The mother to his child—and if truth be known, a mother to Teddy himself. Hell, she had even stuck around after their divorce while he flaunted mistress after mistress at her. Could a woman who did that have killed him?

JB and Len parted company after brunch. Len to practice. JB to rendezvous with Charles.

Five

◈ ◈ ◈ ◈ ◈ ◈ ◈ ◈ ◈ ◈ ◈ ◈ ◈ ◈ ◈ L en was, as usual, about a half hour late for his meeting that afternoon at Lee's house. His lateness was a chronic long term condition that drove JB mad with frustration. Even telling Len an earlier meeting time couldn't cure him. JB swore often and loudly that Len would probably delay his own death. Keeping the Grim Reaper looking at his empty hourglass, tapping a bony foot in aggravation.

He knocked at the door and then hugged Lee when she opened it. Mummered apologies were poo-bahed as she hugged back. Air kisses settled the matter. Len looked around the apartment expecting to see a gaggle of producers and only saw a single person with a garbage bag picking up the debris from the earlier wake.

Lee pointed him to the dining room where the group of

producers and investors were waiting. The earlier buffet had been removed and a sidetable was now in place with a coffee urn and what looked to be the leftover canapés.

There were ten men sitting at the linen covered table , They resembled what most would imagine bank executives look like. Or undertakers. All Brooks Brothered, rep tied, and fluff dried. They looked rather grim as they sat around Lee's table with half eaten demi sandwiches and empty coffee cups in front of them. Buzzards gathering to pick at the bones of Teddy's show? In Len's estimation they had about the same amount of charm as a pack of carrion.

He was introduced and brought a chair. Feeling a bit like a schoolboy in front of the disciplinary board he sat and folded his hands in his lap. Good manners always bred good impressions, as his mama always said.

Then Ronald Prescott, the on-line producer of *Mrs. MacKenzie's Muddle*, stood and called the meeting to order. Ronald was a latter day David Merrick want-a-be, except he was missing the savoir fair of the original Broadway wheeler/dealer. Where Merrick carried off his activities with a certain panache and verve, Ronald Prescott could only manage an overall aura of profound distress. He always seemed to his acquaintances like he was the little Dutch boy holding back a dike full of his own perceived disasters.

His career on Broadway had only served up a couple of fair to middling successes when Teddy Brewster wasn't attached to the project—the two shows he had produced without him made a marginal run of less than a hundred performances each. It was considered a not very spectacular showing and generated talk that Prescott couldn't make it without Teddy. It all weighed heavily on Prescott's much furrowed forehead. That he hadn't had the incipient heart attack or stroke that seemed to bubble under his surface was the real miracle.

As the on-line producer Prescott was the man responsible for all the executive decisions; meaning casting, stage management, set and costume design, advertising, bookings, plus dealing with the unions. It was a huge responsibility and Prescott showed the weight of it in the set of his shoulders and the constant beads of sweat on his forehead. He was perpetually wiping at his brow as he swallowed chalky liquids like chocolate milkshakes.

What was Prescott's main strength was being a genius at the art of penny-pitching. He could wring a turnip from a cornfield if he'd had too. A bookkeeper and nit-picker par-excellance he knew how to raise money and then keep it. This ability guaranteed profits while other productions foundered under the weight of their bottom lines. Ronald Prescott and Teddy Brewster had made large fortunes together. But with Teddy now out of the picture there was worry among the investors about how the show would go on.

Now Prescott was standing at the head of Lee Arden's dining room table. He mopped again at his forehead with an already damp handkerchief, then he pushed his glasses into place on his nose. He spoke to the assembly.

"Gentlemen, we are convened here today to make several decisions necessary to the survival of our current production. Since we have already invested a year and a half in the project and moved perilously close to starting previews we must make these decisions as quickly as possible..."

There were mummers from the men around the table.

"First, I want to put your minds at ease. I have, with the help of other interested parties, accessed the situation, and I put to you that Christopher Brewster, the son of our late director..." Lee could be heard catching a sob. "... has volunteered to assume the reins of *Mrs. MacKenzie's Muddle* for us." He stopped and managed a weak smile in Christopher's direction.

There was polite applause and positive nods from the assembly. They all seemed to approve of the choice. Thus bolstered by their reaction, Ronald went on, "And, as an added incentive to using him, he has secured the personal services of his mother. Of course, we all know that is the great star, Lee Arden. She has agreed to take the lead in our production."

There was a gasp and enthusiastic applause from the group, followed by more mummers of approval running from man to man around the table.

Then, with a gratified smile on his face, Ronald went on. "So, I am suggesting we accept Christopher's most generous offer and turn our show over to him. Will we make that unanimous?"

The group gave an elated acceptance to the plan.

Then Christopher stood and spoke. "Thank you, gentlemen, for your vote of confidence..."

One of the producers at the other end of the table spoke sideways to the man next to him. "With Lee Arden in the lead this could be directed by a monkey and we'd still have a hit."

Christopher went on. "I realize this has been a troubled show so far. My father was a bit like a giant gorilla in a china shop with his plans for the revival of the show. Well, let me assure you all...I am a much smaller monkey. Barely a chimpanzee." Christopher nodded his head at the person who had mentioned simians before. The man slid down in his seat and looked the other way, not meeting Christopher's eye.

"Trust me, gentlemen, I will dampen the more radical changes Teddy was planning for the show. However, I will want to keep the dance numbers he was working on before..." His voice faded as Lee began to sob again. Len took her hand and patted it gently.

Christopher continued, "...with much of the original libretto reinstated, of course. Although, I believe it does need freshening. My mother will step into the lead. That would be bolstered by another casting decision. Our already signed original star, Betty Kane, would now take the part of Lee's sister. I can better see Betty playing a sister rather than a mother. Of course, we would have to rewrite her lines so that she comes off younger and more vivacious. I want her closer to Betty's real persona." This idea again received enthusiastic acceptance from the assembled money men.

"I've asked Betty to arrive after our meeting today so that together we can discuss this new part. I have a feeling she'll be happy to go along with our ideas. Also the re-write will mean Jerry Rosen would now play the part of the sister's fiancée instead of Mrs. MacKenzie's. With that change of character I propose we'll get the same comic repartee from Jerry and Betty as before, but perpetrated by more attractive characters. Plus, having two great stars like Mother and Betty on the same stage should be very exciting..."

Lee spoke up. "Don't get too enthused, boys. I've been gone for quite awhile, you know? This is all contingent on my being able to handle the singing. I don't even know if I can hit the high notes anymore. Or the high kicks for that matter." She then turned on her chair and holding onto the back did just that. Kicked her leg high enough to reach over her head, while still sitting. She got a hearty laugh for her effort.

Christopher went on. "...and Mother appearing with us leads to another stroke of good fortune." Christopher laid his hand on Len's shoulder. "I would like to offer up Mr. Len Matthews..." He gave Len a signal to stand. "... as Lee's love interest in our new production. Jerry, as I said, would now be Betty's partner. I believe Len here will be more suitable as Lee's suitor. And he has just proven himself as the lead in a musical that recently closed out of town. An unfortunate event, but it has made him available to us. He would be perfect as our Mr. VanRoddy, don't you think?" Christopher stepped aside, leaving Len to face the producers.

Ronald spoke up, "I certainly agree with Christopher on this. I hope you all will too..."

One of the men asked, "Can he sing?"

Len said, "I can, although it leans toward what Rex Harrison did in *Fair Lady*. Or Richard Burton in *Camelot*. A rhythmic speaking of the lyric." He gave a shrug and smiled. "Hey, it worked for Katherine Hepburn in *Coco*."

Christopher stepped back beside Len. "It should mesh nicely with Lee's lower register. Which I propose we audition for all of you right now." Christopher turned to Len. "Would you be willing to sing with Lee?"

They both took up the cue and agreed. The group of producers didn't have to know that Lee and Len had discussed what they might sing on the way into the meeting. They had decided the duet from the close of Act II was safely in their range. And it was familiar to all of them since the recording by Tony Bennett had topped the charts for ten weeks back in nineteen-sixty-one.

The men all rose and went out to the white living room while Len and Lee stood together by the piano. Len placed his hands on Lee's shoulders and whispered, "You're my star. I'll follow you to the heavens." She placed a hand on his and patted, "I'll try not to lead us right into a black hole?"

The romantic duet went over well. Christopher played piano, noodleing notes as the two of them found their way through the song. Len's voice found a sweet harmony with Lee's growl of a contralto. She had never had a strong voice, even at her peak, but keeping it in a lower octave served her nicely. She was able to reach the higher notes comfortably which gave a rousing emphasis to the rest of the song. A sort of Lisa Kirk crossed with Carol Channing charm gave great style to her delivery. With proper micing in the theater she would have the audiences peeing in their seats. And the two of them, Len and Lee, looked very good together. They made a quite passable and attractive couple.

Len was officially offered the part of VanRoddy on the strength of that single song. Len, for his part, was vastly relieved. He had auditioned for *Hook and Wendy* ten separate times before a decision was made. Audition's were the bane of every actor's life. They provided the battlefield where actors must fight their own personal wars. Pitting their fragile sensibilities against the callus unfeeling enemy—the casting director. Walk into a room where you've received a call back and find thirty other actors that all look like you waiting to see the same casting person. The one who had assured you that you were their number one choice. Crushed ego, anyone? Len certainly knew about that. Getting this part offered in this manner meant another step up for him on the Broadway ladder. It would bring him to a point where scripts would be sent to him. He wouldn't have to scrabble so hard for work. Rehearsals on *Mrs. MacKenzie's Muddle* would resume the next week.

While the investor gentlemen gathered their coats and congratulated themselves on keeping the show alive, Len and Lee sat at the piano and softly sang together. They were already working on their parts—finding their voices, blending them, seeing what worked and what didn't.

"This is going to be great, Lee. We'll wow em."

"I hope so."

That's when Betty and Roger arrived at the front door. Christopher hurried over to meet them, walked them down the stairs, and with his arm around Betty's waist, led them off into another room. Lee waved at them, then watched with interest as they disappeared into the den. She turned back to Len. "You know, this might work. She is certainly a star. But I've heard she's terrible to work with. She'll upstage us right, left, backwards and forwards. The lady is a scene stealer from way back."

Len chuckled. "Hey, that didn't keep Bette Davis from working with Miriam Hopkins. More than once at that. Anyway, I won't let her get away with much of that sort of folderol. We'll keep her in check. You can bet your butt, I will."

"And Roger too? That latest husband of hers is like a mongoose on a cobra if anyone crosses Betty."

"At her direction from what I hear. He's like a spider waiting to be eaten by his mate."

"But that's impossible. Betty's a strict vegetarian. Don't you know that?" Lee was teasing. Betty Kane was notorious about what she would or would not eat. Only certain foods were allowed to pass her lips. She was known to even take plastic containers of her special foods into restaurants.

"Well, Roger doesn't look to have much meat on him, does he? She could have him for lunch. And I'm sure she has once or twice."

Lee giggled.

"But seriously Lee. With what Christopher says he has planned—you two women on stage and with a totally new production around you—I can't see how this show can miss. This one has hit written all over it." Len rubbed his hands together. "And it means I'll get to work with you, darling. That's the best part of it. I've wanted us to get together ever since we did that first benefit. You remember? The first Broadway Cares?"

Broadway Cares/Equity Fights AIDS was the theatrical community reacting to the epidemic as early as nineteen-eighty-two. Way before AMFAR, which had started just the previous year. Liz Taylor had created her group out West soon after Rock Hudson passed. But New York actors had early on banded together to raise funds for their many comrades and fellow performers who were being afflicted by the disease. Broadway Cares/Equity Fights AIDS was born out of that concern. Benefit performances, yard sales on Shubert Alley, star-studded auctions, you name it and the Broadway community had responded. It made one proud to be in the profession. He and Lee had done several of the benefits over the past few years, always having great fun working together. Now, if they could transfer that feeling to their roles in *Mrs. Mackenzie* they could be well on their way to Tony nominations.

Lee and Len worked for another ten minutes. They stopped when Betty and Christopher emerged from their meeting with the news that Betty had agreed to take the secondary part in the production. That occasioned hugs and congratulations all around. Len then let the two of them do the same thing he and Lee had been doing—begin working on their parts and relationships. To that end he excused himself. The entire meeting had taken several hours which, of course, made him late, again, for the dinner engagement he was going to. The one he hadn't mentioned to JB at brunch.

He was meeting the dancer he had talked to at the wake that morning. Jimmy was his name. Jimmy Jameson. Len didn't know much about him, but he was very charming, quite handsome, and had bluntly asked Len out for dinner that evening. And why not, Len figured? It wasn't like he had a full calendar. His social statistics of late were close to zero. It had a lot to do with him just having returned from the road. While he was out of town most of his friends went on with their regular lives, without including or thinking about him. Now that he was back they still just didn't think of putting him back into their schedules. And as for himself, he had been busy trying to scrounge up work; so the entertainment part of his life had been basically put on a backburner. That meant he had been walking the single side of life for the last month or so. Well, except for JB, he was always there, but even he'd been busy with his own projects. Len lately had found himself spending most of his nights in front of the TV and eating frozen dinners. So, if this very attractive man wanted to spend time with him, who was he to deny him. It might be fun, and it was a chance to get out.

Len grabbed a taxi and headed for the theater district. Getting out at Forty-fourth Street he aimed directly for Sardi's, a renowned gathering place for actors and the like. Also famous for the caricatures that hung on the walls. A bit of an old-fashioned choice of restaurant Len was thinking, but it might be a hoot to see the old place. He hadn't been there in ages.

He spotted Jimmy already there and standing at the bar. He went over and touched his shoulder. Jimmy turned and smiled. It was quite dazzling. Gorgeous white even teeth almost sparked in the light. His smile lit up his whole face. A very handsome man in the Alec Baldwin mold. Cleft chin, square jaw, compact muscular frame, thick thighs, as would be expected with a dancer.

Jimmy explained that he had already left their names at the desk and there would be a wait, did he want something to drink? He signaled the barkeep.

"You need to move down a couple of seats..." Len said. "...that way we're closer to the cheese pot."

"The what?"

"Right there." Len pointed. "It's the best part of this old place." He shifted and reached for the free pot of cheese Sardi's put out for its patrons. He dipped a knife into the communal pot. He slathered a good sized dollop on a cracker and savored the sharp gooey cheddar. "I've made quite a few meals out of this cheese. Before I could afford to actually eat here. When I was still struggling."

They chatted for ten minutes or so and were then called for thier table. They settled in a booth and looked to see whose pictures were on the wall above thier heads. Len had Helen Hayes. Jimmy had Alfred Drake. Old guard show people. Their waiter, who looked as if he'd been there since Al Jolson was a star, took their orders and shuffled off.

"Can you imagine the opening nights and stars that man has seen?"

"Forget him. What about you? You've been in the spotlight forever. What stories you must be able to tell..." Jimmy let this trail off as he realized what he'd said.

"Well, Laurette Taylor had already retired when I got

here, so it hasn't been all that long," Len said.

"No. No. That isn't what I meant at all. What I mean is I'm more interested in your stories than in that waiters. Gosh, I'm so sorry. Can we start over?"

Len chuckled. "Of course, no offense taken. God, I have been trudging these streets for eons at that..." That led easily to conversation and a more than pleasant meal. Len dominated the conversation with his stories and Jimmy played the acolyte, listening raptly.

Len was flattered the man was so interested, but did turn the tables at one point and ask, "So, what do you have planned for your life? Are you going to end up like most dancers teaching kids in some small town?"

"Actually, I have another cliché in mind. I'm going to become an antique's dealer. I'll planning on opening my own store." He went on to explain that *Mrs. MacKenzie* was going to be his last show. That he had applied for a loan to finance the dream and was waiting for the bank to answer. Soon, he hoped.

Conversation continued over coffee and in the cab on the way to Len's apartment.

ix

◆◆◆◆◆◆◆◆◆◆◆◆◆◆Charles
shared some primo weed on the way over to the club. By
the time he and JB arrived at *The Candle II*, the mellow
was just settling in.

Several parked motorcycles in a line and leather clad
men standing out front might lead one to think the event
that night was for the S&M crowd. The recently closed *Anvil*
guys had found a new venue to play their kinky games in.
Instead it was *The NY Jacks* holding their session inside.
Those leather boys were probably props hired by the bar
to make an impression. *The Jacks,* however, was open to
all gay persuasions as long as the rules were kept in mind.
Rule number one: *No lips below the hips*.

Inside, JB paid his member's admission, bought his

drink tickets, and stripped to his jockstrap, leather vest, and recently purchased barracks cap. He greeted a couple of friends on his way to the bar, and got ready for the night ahead. It would prove to be a revelation.

Above the bar a loft had been built for the use of the patrons. It had at the moment its light fixtures either off or down on dim, so there were shadows of wagon wheel chandeliers breaking up what light did exist. The effect was designed to create a hyper butch masculine atmosphere for the men. At least what movies and cigarette advertising told us was butch and masculine. There was a rough cowboy feel filling the air. The shadows were also a place for couples or groups to form and explore their same sex desires. All within the rules of the club, of course. About sixty-five men filled the straw covered area while JB sat on a bench against the wall and watched.

JB was sitting comfortably observing the activity between two men he recognized as models from the previous months issue of *GQ Magazine*. They were entwined and appreciating each other as much as JB was reciprocating. That these beautiful young men had come together for JB's viewing pleasure and satisfaction was both voluptuous and sensual. Satisfying for all parties concerned—thank you very much.

Then JB looked for a moment beyond the scene going on in front of him. He spotted a beauty standing against the wall behind the two men. Who can explain what it is that will grab at a man's libido? But over there, leaning against the planked wall, was one who did it for JB. Grab at his libido that is. He could grab his other parts on his own. JB felt his cock lengthen.

JB watched as the light picked out the play of muscles on the beauty's body. Beauty's hand was distractedly massaging the thin line of hair leading from his navel into the red colored thong at his hips. An outlined almost graphic bulge was lying against his thigh. JB felt himself drawn to this man standing across from him wearing little more than a cowboy hat and boots. He was like a bear to trout. Why shouldn't he be, the man standing there was living porn.

JB moved from his bench to stand in front of this beautiful man. He raised his hand and slowly laid it on the man's chest. The man's left nipple caught between JB's two fingers. He twisted gently. Beauty's head, in shadow by the brim of his hat, shifted slightly to indicate JB's presence. Beauty's mouth and jaw were etched, almost cartoon like, in the dim light. JB saw Beauty's lip curve upward in a tight smile. Then Beauty lifted a single finger to his hat, acknowledging JB's interest. Not a word was spoken.

JB's finger reached out once again to Beauty's nipple. He began to rub around the dark nib, and felt it harden under his touch. JB heard Beauty catch his breath. He smiled.

Then Beauty reached out and laid his own hand on JB's chest, repeating JB's action. JB caught his own breath at the sensation. Keeping the lips and hips rule in mind JB leaned forward and flicked his tongue at Beauty's neck, shifting his own hat backward as he did. He began to lick at the man's neck hallow, then moved over to the clavicle, stopping at his shoulder. Then he reversed it, taking his mouth and tongue back to Beauty's chest. JB moved his head down and licked at the still stiffened nipple. In reaction, Beauty's head rolled to the side lazily as he moaned a satisfied growl.

JB knew then. The two of them would go on to know each other. They would explore, desire, rise, and peak together.

Twenty-five minutes later the two men, finding themselves ready, moved in closer, making their cocks meet. Beauty's round veined eight inches began to pulsate in JB's hand; soon enough hot jism poured from the blood red head. His cum fell scalding upon JB's dick waiting beneath. JB moaned as he wrapped his hand on his own cock and using Beauty's spilled cum as a lubricant jerked himself to his own finish. His stomach began to raffle and he shot his load against Beauty's hard stomach.

◆◆◆

A satisfied smile on his face, his breathing returning to normal, JB knew he had to find out the identify of this person he was leaning against. This man's mere presence, with a single touch, had been able to bring him to such pleasure he felt as if his head had exploded. Reaching up

55

to lift the brim of the cowboy hat JB's surprise quickly changed to delight. He had just had an encounter with Christopher Brewster.

Hadn't it only been that morning that they had spoken? And JB had thought him beautiful then. However, since lusting at a wake being pretty much on the tacky side JB had been prevented from cruising the man. But JB also knew that Christopher Brewster was a hunk, no two ways about it. He was simply gorgeous.

Christopher smiled and leaned in, giving JB a serious kiss, with tongues intertwining, saliva exchanged. That soon led to them going downstairs where they dressed and left the club with the intention of exploring each other's more uncharted territories at Christopher's Westside apartment. Luckily it was within walking distance.

The chill in the night air made their breath fog as they walked side by side from Broadway toward Columbus Avenue. A couple of blocks over from where they'ed had that morning's conversation at Lee's apartment, found them now climbing a four story set of stairs to enter a pre-war studio done up in late-hippie style. Most of the furniture was to JB's eyes, pickups from the trash. New York being the best place ever for trash picks. Native New Yorkers wait anxiously for their weekly trash days. That's when people moving from their apartments leave behind their unwanteds. Rugs, lamps, chairs. You name it.

Many of the pieces Christopher would later say were donations from the sets of shows he had directed. The furniture being covered with Native American weavings went with the vaguely Southwest/Calif rustic decorating style. It was a coast too far from its home, but it was intimately romantic once it had been candlelit.

Christopher and JB quickly found the bed and opened themselves to each other.

Lips and hips indeed.

even

◆◆◆◆◆◆◆◆◆◆◆◆◆◆◆◆◆◆The next morning, Len, in his robe, was puttering in the efficiency kitchen. Making toast and coffee for him and Jimmy.

Okay, Len was thinking as he put the crystals in the cups, it was a nice enough night. Nothing spectacular. Adequate sex. No fireworks though. Jimmy seems a pleasant enough young man. Well, he's not pre-pubescent, but younger than I am. And the conversation between us was spectacular. We just sparked and gabbed for hours after we'd finished with the sex. It was fun. Jumping from subject to subject. Jimmy's mind making the same leaps as his did.

Finally they had drifted off for a few hours of sleep.

One of the things they had in common was the antique's

thing. Le (especially since he had gotten sober) hit the thrift stores and antique shops on a regular basis. Picking up odd bits and pieces that appealed to him. His place was filling up with bric-a-brac—called smalls in the trade. He'd even taken a night course at the New School on the subject of collectibles. Vintage tins were a favorite of his, also nice pieces of glass. And after his recent trip to Denver he had several pieces of Indian art—a few pueblo pots, a Hopi Kachina, a good Navajo rug—that sort of thing. Now, Jimmy was wandering around the apartment looking over his tchotchkes.

"You have some nice things...," he said, picking up a pillow with an Atlantic City sham from the 1940's Len had found for two dollars. He replaced it on the chair it sat in then came over to the doorway to the tiny kitchen.

"Especially this."

He was talking about the Deco bar Len had picked up at an auction several months before and placed across the doorway.

"Thirties, right? A wonderful period. And you can still get pieces for practically nothing."

"You like it? I thought it worked great for storage in here. Of course, I paid too much..."

"That always happens when you find just the right piece. This is very nice though."

"And it's a fake. I didn't realize it when I bought it though."

"Really. It's a good one. I have to admit I don't have a lot of experience with the period. So I could have been fooled just like you."

Len set the plate of toast on top of the bar. Jimmy grabbed a piece and took a bite. "Oh, what's that?" He went over by the door and picked up a cane that stood in a Majolica urn. He inspected it. "Silver tip and ferrule. Ebony wood. This is good, Len."

"Really? I got it at the flea market in Soho. For only a few bucks. Twenty, I think. I used it as a prop in one of my last plays. I liked it because of the top with the comedy and tragedy masks. I thought it was cool."

"You know what. There's a makers mark here on the bottom ferrule. I could have it checked out for you. See who the mark belongs to. I think this is old. And it might be worth something. Let me take it with me. I'll let you know what I find out."

"Sure. You think it might be worth more than I paid for it?"

"I do."

"Then definitely check it out. What do you want to do today? I have the whole day. I don't start rehearsals until Thursday."

"Maybe you don't. I have a one o'clock call. A chorus boys work is never done."

"Then we'll do something another time."

"You bet."

JB and Christopher spent the morning wanting only to be with each other and satisfy their raging libidos. Christopher even managed to spend that first day alone with JB. The entire day was spent together in his apartment. Most of the time they were in bed making love, except when munching from the refrigerator or ordering from the deli downstairs.

There was also a short time when JB did Christopher a favor and sat up to look over the script of *Mrs. MacKenzie's Muddle*. Christopher had asked him to give some advice on the changes he wanted to work on the plot.

Since his mother had read JB's novels Christopher was at least familiar with who JB was. He knew what JB did for a living, including his having written a Broadway play, been nominated for a Tony, and won an Obie.

Christopher wanted to know how possible it was to change the mother to a sister and add a sub-plot between her and the originally cast VanRoddy. Then to use a younger man as Lee's love interest. Would it work?

Surprisingly, after a quick read-through, JB thought it could. A love affair between the two couples would even give room for some farcical elements to be worked in—mistaken identities and the like. If the Elizabethans and Defoe could do it why not an American Broadway musical?

Dance: Ten

ight

◆◆◆◆◆◆◆◆◆◆◆◆Rehearsals started that next Thursday. Which meant JB and Christopher had to curtail their lust for each other some, since there were fewer chances for them to meet. Both were busy, Christopher most of all.

Rehearsals for the cast of *Mrs. MacKenzie* were like starting over from scratch for the company. It only took a morning meeting to realize Teddy had managed to get only a few numbers choreographed before his death. He'd done the opening, a second act finale and some scene transitions for his dance opera idea.

That opening, however, was a lollapalooza. It was possibly the best work Teddy had ever done for the stage. Tambourines and all it was a terrific routine that managed to introduce the characters and state the theme for the evening all in one exciting seven minute dance and song number. It was sure to have the audience on the edge of their seats, applauding before it was even over. It needed to be used exactly as it stood, not only because of it striking the perfect note for the show, but it would stand as a tribute to Teddy. It would be his last completed piece.

There did need to be one change, however. The new VanRoddy, Len, had to be worked in. To that end Christopher had recruited Jillian Morgan, Teddy's dance assistant. Or ex-mistress, whichever you prefer.

She was asked to use her knowledge of Teddy's work to get Len introduced into the routine. She took over, created the extra steps needed in exactly Teddy's style, and Len was slipped in seamlessly. That got her the job of working out the rest of the dances for the show. And she did a bang up job of it. She and Christopher—with Lee as their advisor— working together, were able to pound out all the dance numbers needed. There ended up being three more major numbers, including a vaudeville takeoff for Betty Kane to tap her way thorough.

The dance numbers would be cause for many arguments between the creators, as will often happen when different creative types work together. Rogers and Hart were notoriously combative. As were Gilbert and Sullivan. Don't even ask about Fosse and his directors. Question's were raised and argued over. Was it too much dance? Or not enough song? Or vice-versa. When Christopher and Jillian would end up at loggerheads it was Lee who would step in and quietly suggest a solution that usually solved the problem.

The dances became a mish-mash of Teddy's older steps recycled by Jillian to look new. It gave the show a nostalgic turn that would appeal to audiences, and it meant the show would still carry Teddy's credit as choreographer on the programs. They judiciously held back on it being a complete dance show, added more traditional elements, and made it Broadway musical in style and tone. Jillian got a *Additional dances staged by* credit for her work.

Len and Lee Arden, along with Betty Kane and her partner Jerry, were called often for private rehearsals, held without the chorus. Betty, being her usual blazingly flamboyant self swanned and swooned all over the stage. She merrily upstaged her little heart out, working desperately to turn every scene into her own private Tony winner. Looks were exchanged between Len and Lee, but for the moment they let her go on with her flamingo dance. Len assured Lee that it wouldn't be a problem when they played.

"What are you going to do?"

Len even managed an angelic look as he said, "Me? I'll just get her under control. I have my ways. You'll see."

Christopher, more concerned with other matters, was moving all over creation in his efforts to bring the show together. As a result he didn't pay much attention to this little bit of discord between his actors. Actors, dances, music, costumes, sets, writing, all of it had to be vetted and approved by both Christopher and Ronald Prescott.

It wasn't an easy task taking on someone else's production. It was made more difficult since the cast and chorus, even the crew, was made up of mostly Teddy's cadre of people. Christopher was an unknown quantity to everyone. There was some reluctance at first, some *but Teddy wouldn't have done it this way* talk.

Christopher, being as diplomatic as he could be under the circumstances, announced to the assembled company the obvious—that Teddy was no longer the director, he was. If they didn't want to follow where he was going then the street was just out the door at the top of the aisle. Then a copy of an interoffice memo was mysteriously hung on the callboard for all to see. It stated there had been seven hundred and fifty-six dancers at the first open auditions for this show. Would they need to call another audition? The dissenters got in line.

Christopher, to make things more complicated, also was dealing with his desire to be with JB. They had gone on from their meeting at *The NY Jacks* to a nicely hot and heavy secret affair. A call to JB when Christopher had an hour to spare would lead them to having frantic sex in the afternoons. Calls from Christopher to JB when his day ended would find them having four hour conversations and, often, a late night visit from JB to Christopher's place.

It also meant JB heard about the trials of putting on

the show from Christopher and then again from Len. They both were telling him things Judy and Mickey had never even thought about. JB knew the show's troubles so well that when Christopher asked him to come on board as a writer it wasn't a surprise.

JB agreed to work on the script for a one time payment until it was performed at the first preview. He was hired only as a consultant not as a credited book writer. That title belonged to the original librettist. JB was simply a freelancer tweaking the script so it was brought up to date and would fulfill the director's vision. What was euphemistically called a show doctor.

◈◈◈

Christopher finally heard about the actors duel with Betty by way of JB, who had gotten the particulars from Len. They had to laugh at the solution Len had devised.

It happened at the first rehearsal where the costume people were able to provide skirts of the proper Eighteen-seventy's period for the ladies. Each of the makeshift skirts had the correct draping that was used in the musicals setting. The skirts were provided so that Lee and Betty could work with the fabrics. So that in performance they would move naturally. As naturally as the corseting, long trains, and heavy fabrics that were a part of the period would allow. The rehearsal skirts were made of a heavy muslin and draped so they were the same weight and length as the more opulent velvet versions they would wear in actual performance.

"Othello's asshole! This thing must weigh forty pounds!" Betty was well known for her colorful Shakespearean curses. She was grousing after hanging the skirt on her hips.

"The weight is as exact as we'll be using for your real costume."

This came from the apprentice sent to deliver the articles to the actors. Poor thing.

Betty marched right up to the young girl and stared her down like a Marine drill sergeant.

"Honey, have you ever heard of using lighter fabrics to simulate the right period? As performers we can act as if the dress weighs fifty pounds. I'll use this for now, but talk to your boss. I want this changed to something more comfortable."

The girl, properly instructed, ran off stage to report Betty's demands to the costumier. And probably to have a proper cry too.

Christopher, his voice coming from somewhere out in the stalls, asked his actors to gather at their marks.

Lee, swishing the bottom of her skirt behind her as she walked, said to Len, "You know there was a whole language of the train back in the Eighteen-hundreds. The way it was held or dragged was supposed to indicate a woman's availability to a suitor." She flipped open a fan she was also practicing with.

Len said, "Men had it much easier. We just had to wear a green carnation to indicate a preference. That came from Oscar Wilde. He was supposed to have been wearing the flower when he got nicked."

Betty standing next to Len laughed. "Was that the name of the boy he was on at the time? Nick?"

Len turned on her. "The man was arrested and pilloried for following what were simply his natural inclinations. How's that for injustice?"

"Oh, sweet Shakespeare's spit! Your one of those bleeding heart gay liberationists." She turned and huffily started to walk away from Len.

As she did Len took a step of his own and deliberately put his foot on her train. Betty continued on unaware of this and when she met resistance pulled against it. Len's leg slid forward an inch or so from her effort. Len then put both feet on the ruffled train. Betty, still trying for a forward trajectory, was stopped cold in a runner's pose. Leaning forward, arms pumping, looking back. She finally stopped, stood straight, and with her arms crossed, stared at Len.

Len smiled sweetly back. "Now, get this, Miss Kane, this is exactly what will happen at every performance of this play I am working with you if you don't rein yourself in. Enough with the flapping all over the stage while Lee and I do our scenes. Do you understand?"

Betty looked at Len's feet and then at his determined face. "I get it..."

"If what your doing doesn't feel right, find your acting chops again, woman. Make it work."

And so rehearsals went.

JB's and Christopher's affair went along with the same sort of bumps and humps. Each was so thoroughly enthralled with the other they wanted only to rip off their clothes and lie together, entwined, body to body for days on end. But because Christopher was so preoccupied with the show it was definitely a challenge for them to get together at all. It was managed however. Managed with stolen moments in the theaters second lobby bathroom and spur of the moment assignations at Christopher's apartment. JB could light the candles at Christopher's place in two minutes flat. He'd timed himself.

It was after one of these afternoon delights that JB was waiting at the door for Christopher to finish getting dressed. Both had appointments to get to. To arrest his pique at Christopher's lingering JB started straightening out the pile of mail lying on the hall table. While stacking the letters by size—JB could be compulsive that way—he found the unopened envelope containing a copy of the autopsy report on Teddy Brewster sent by the police.

JB looked up at Christopher coming from the bedroom. He held up the unopened envelope. "You didn't read this?"

"Teddy had a heart attack. What more do I need to know?"

JB was opening the flap. Then he lifted out the page of white paper he found inside. "This is a copy of the preliminary report. How did you get this. The police don't give these out willy-nilly."

Christopher stopped at the hall mirror and began tying his tie.

"One of the perks of being a celebrity. Things just become available. Well?"

"Acute myocardial infarction."

"Which is?"

"A heart attack."

"Now can we go?"

"I don't get it Christopher. Why don't you care? Your father could have been a victim here."

"Teddy was always a victim."

"You two never got along. Did you?"

"JB...," Christopher stopped tying his tie and turned to him. "...I am a child of celebrities. In most normal families when a child comes into their lives he gets to be the star. All the attention is on him. But when you're the kid of two famous people they get to stay the stars. I had to fight for every beam of light I could get to shine on me. It was a war, JB." He turned back to the mirror. "Now, can we go? I have to watch Betty and Mom try to make a scene out of this dreck we have for a script."

JB said, "Maybe you want another script doctor. I hear Neil Simon is available."

"At the kind of money he would want? You've got the job, kiddo. Just make it sparkle." He leaned forward and kissed JB's cheek.

JB opened the door. Christopher stepped out and set the locks.

◆ ◆ ◆

Jimmy was saying, "So I gave Doctor Stark your cane. He called me yesterday and said he had something interesting to tell me about it."

"Like what?"

They were walking on Madison Avenue in the Sixties. When they got to a stairway going to a second floor business Jimmy turned. Along the wall next to the stairway were several plaques, one of which advertised the antique shop of Dr. Milton Stark, PHD. Jimmy continued, "I have no idea. The doctor just asked me to come by. He's upstairs." He began to climb the stairs.

Len followed and on the first landing went through a glass and aluminum door into the shop on the right. A little bell rang as the door opened. A man sitting at a rolltop desk looked up, stood, and came toward them. "Hello, hello." The shop was small and crammed with tables topped with old crocheted scarf's and various other antiques; stacks of plates and dinnerware, glass and decanter sets, porcelain bowls, statuary, and the like. Shelves lined the walls holding more of the same. The doctor was a middle aged man with a Van Dyke beard, thick glasses, a tweed suit, and a bad polyester wig in a Beatles cut. "Jimmy," he said,

"I'm so glad you came by. Come, come, let me show you what I've discovered." He had an accent, maybe British, but it seemed put on to Len. An affectation or maybe prep school he was thinking.

Jimmy introduced Len and they followed the man over to the desk. Beside it was a table from which the doctor picked up Len's cane. He fondled it as he continued speaking. "This has turned out to be a very interesting artifact. You said that it was picked up at a flea market?"

Len answered. "That's right. A few years ago. I was looking for a prop to use for a part I was playing. A gentleman in a period piece. I liked the decoration on the top. The comedy and tragedy masks. I thought it was perfect for an actor."

"Indeed, indeed," the doctor said. "Well, that was true when it was originally purchased too. Let me explain." He sat at his desk and rummaged through the papers there. "I was able to find the owner of the makers mark you noticed on the ferrule, Jimmy. It belongs to..." He picked up a piece of paper. "Yes, here it is. Ovington Benedict. He was a silversmith and jeweler here in New York City during the Eighteen-sixties. He was a partner with his brother in a store at One-seventy-one Broadway until Eighteen-seventy. He made this cane sometime in that period."

"You mean that cane is over a hundred years old?" Len was flabbergasted.

"Correct. And I was able to do much more research than I expected. It turns out that the Museum of The City of New York has, on microfilm, copies of the original ledgers from Benedict Brothers, the shop Ovington was affiliated with. Were you aware this cane has a monogram?"

Len was surprised. "It does? I've never found one."

The doctor held out the cane. "It's just under the top, where the ebony and the silver connect. Look..."

Len took the cane and inspected it. And there it was. In a tiny engraved script were the initials JWB. "I see them. I had no idea those were there."

The doctor was getting excited now. "Do you have any idea who JWB might have been?"

"Not a clue. Do you?"

"As a matter of fact. When I inspected the ledgers at the museum I went all the way back to when the store opened in

Eighteen-sixty. When I got to March of Eighteen-sixty-two, I found a very interesting entry. This entry..." He held out a photocopy of a ledger page. He had highlighted a section that read in the florid handwriting used by people of that era. "Ebony and silver cane. Tip cast as comedy/tragedy. Engraved JWB. Special order for actor Booth. Forty-eight dollars."

"Booth?" Len looked at the doctor.

"A little bit more research uncovered the fact that the actor John Wilkes Booth had his New York debut in March of Eighteen-sixty-two. A coincidence? I don't think it is."

"You mean to tell me that this cane was made for John Wilkes Booth. The man who killed Lincoln?"

"All the evidence points to it. You have made a very important find, sir."

"You're joking."

The doctor went on. "Forty-eight dollars was a great deal of money in the Eighteen-sixties. Booth must have bought the cane with the money he had earned from his debut. The cane was probably meant to commemorate the event. That's explains the theatrical theme of the cap."

Jimmy asked, "How much would the cane be worth now, doctor?"

"Very hard to be sure. Not a lot of Booth's personal effects come to the market. But collectors of Civil War memorabilia would certainly be interested. At a good auction I would imagine you could get between six and eight thousand for it."

"Oh, my God." Len sat in a upholstered horsehair dining chair that sat beside the desk. "I can't believe it. This? I only paid twenty bucks for it."

"A bit more research might be necessary. If a picture could be found with Booth holding the cane it would cinch it. But all indications make it genuine."

Jimmy and Len thanked the doctor and left the shop. Len's hand had begun to hurt from the grip he was holding on to the cane with. He loosened it and flexed his fingers. Eight thousand dollars? Eight thousand dollars!

It only took them a few minutes to walk down the stairs from the shop and find a cafe where they slid into a booth facing each other.

"I don't believe it. So much money for this?"

"Aren't you lucky, Len. Are you going to sell it?"

"I don't know what I'm going to do. I'm still in shock."

"What a windfall for you. I could have used one like it."

"What do you mean, Jimmy?"

"The loan I was waiting for?" Len nodded. "I was turned down. The bank was reluctant to loan such a large amount to finance a retired dancer in an antique store. So, I'm not going to be able to open after all."

"How much were you asking for?"

"Ten thousand. It doesn't seem like much does it? Particularly when you think that that cane there is worth eight. But they wouldn't give it to me."

"Oh, Jimmy, I'm sorry. I know it meant a lot to you."

"Len, what are the chances of you loaning it to me? I know we have a very short relationship but would you consider it?"

Len blanched and hemmed and hawed a bit.

"I'll pay you interest, Len. Ten percent. That's more than the bank was asking. And consider it a business arrangement. You would have a share of the business for your contribution. It would help a lot, Len."

"Jimmy, that's a great deal of money. I have to think on it. I'll let you know. Okay?"

He agreed, but looked a bit disappointed.

ine

It
was at dinner that evening with Len when JB pulled out
the autopsy report on Teddy Brewster he had slipped into
his pocket that afternoon.

On closer reading it was still true that it was a heart
attack that had killed the famous dancer, but there were a
couple of anomalies too. There were crystalline remnants
of amyl-nitrite found lodged in the inner mucus lining of
Teddy's nostrils. Nitrites leave behind a residue from the
inhaling of them. And that was found in Teddy's nostrils?
Why?

"Len, it doesn't make sense. Why would a man who had
just had heart surgery be inhaling a substance that makes
the organ beat faster. He was lucky he had any pulse at

all."

Len looked up from his menu. "Oh, JB, please. His snorting poppers had nothing to do with his death. His bypass didn't work. It's as imple as that."

"I think it does. It could be that someone wanted Teddy out of the way. So they put amyl-nitrite in that inhaler he had in his hand to accomplish just that."

"JB, put these three words in order. Goose, chase, and wild. Your reaching for a murder where there isn't any."

JB was barely paying attention. "You know what, I think I'll go see Lieutenant Kelly tomorrow. Run my suspicions pass him."

"And whom will you accuse?"

"I have no idea. There are a couple of possibilities."

"You're not going to implicate Lee Arden are you? There is no way..."

"No. I admit I considered her at first. I decided she wouldn't have. For one thing, she was with us when it happened. You saw her reaction. She was in total shock at his death. She definitely didn't know he was going to die. But you know who wasn't shocked?"

"Who?"

"Christopher. He was the most impassive son I've ever seen. Not a sign of grieving."

"That could have been shock too. It effects different people differently."

"True, I guess." JB thought for a moment. "You know, for Teddy to take a hit from that inhaler it would have had to be loaded with the amyl before he used it. Right? That indicates pre-meditation. Someone would have had to plan for him to have the inhaler in his procession. Which, whoever that person might be, knew would kill him..."

"Well, stoic or not I can't believe that you suspect Christopher..."

"What? No, not really. Then again, he did have motive..." JB shook his head. "No. I'm not convinced. He couldn't have. "

"Good." Len, feeling particularly sneaky right then, put a spur of the moment plan into action. He had suspected there was something going on with JB and the director for weeks now, but wasn't sure exactly what. This turn in the conversation might give him a chance to find out what it was. "Because, being the horny sex starved pervert I am has me thinking I might ask Christopher out. Actually, he's one of a couple of the cast members I could be interested in." Len waited a moment for that to sink in. He was wondering how it would go over.

JB stopped his glass midway to his mouth.

Len smiled at him and put his hands together under his chin. Fluttering his eyelashes, he said, "Do you think he'll say yes?"

JB set down his drink.

"Len, you know to be honest, I'm not at all positive he would. I'm not so sure that you would be his type. You might be better off chasing after someone else."

"Why? You think I'm too old for him?"

"No, no. Not at all. He's fully grown. Over the age of consent. As are you. What I mean is that he hasn't said he's gay. And if he is, he's not out. You might not be the right gender. What if he's already seeing someone else?"

"He's very discrete then. There haven't been any indications. No sappy grins. No gooey phone calls." Len placed a napkin on his lap. "Then again, there have been a few instances where he's disappeared during an afternoon rehearsal. You don't suppose..."

"Well, there you go. Of course he's seeing someone. He has a girlfriend. Some sweet young thing I'll bet."

"You're probably right. What a shame. He is such a pretty boy, isn't he?. I mean I'd be willing to make broth from his jockey shorts and have it for lunch."

The waiter arrived with their food.

While they ate JB silently congratulated himself on his handling of Len's interest in Christopher. He had needed to give Len as little as he could on the subject while still heading him off in some other direction. Christopher had asked him specifically to keep their meetings together a secret. He said he didn't want the papers splashing his personal business all over their pages. With Teddy's death, along with the rest of the publicity it had generated, it could easily happen. So Christopher, because of his job on *Mrs. MacKenzie's Muddle*, was under heavy press scrutiny right then. The papers would have loved to report on a gay love nest, now wouldn't they? Besides, they both figured why shouldn't they keep it to themselves? What business was it of the press, or anyone else for that matter?

And if JB was completely honest with himself, the subterfuge added a slight scent of danger to their assignations. A bit of spice. Like if James Bond was making it with OddJob. JB and Christopher were already hot for each other; their sweaty clutching at each other when they would meet proved that. The danger of exposure just made it that much better.

Ten

"I think your looking for something that isn't there, Bent. Not that I don't appreciate your trying to help with the case, but what you've telling me is made out of gauze. The man had a heart attack after a long history of heart problems. Isn't that enough?"

Lieutenant Kelly of the NYPD homicide squad rolled his chair over to a file cabinet in his glass walled office.

"We don't make cases where there is no indication of foul play."

He put away the file he had been looking at.

"What about the nitrites in his nostrils?" JB asked. "That's an indication of something, isn't it?"

"That the vic did poppers. It's not uncommon, Bent. You

can buy the little brown bottles from almost any newsstand in Manhattan."

"Not when the person buying them just had heart surgery, Kelly. If he did use them by choice then his death should be ruled a suicide. Maybe you people can investigate that? A possible suicide?"

Kelly straightened some papers on his desk. Shaking his head he said, "Your still reaching, Bent. You need to find me some solid evidence as to why there was a attempt on Teddy Brewster's life. Then I'll look into it. Now get the hell out of here. I have work to do."

JB left, but was completely dissatisfied. with the result of his meeting. The police weren't going to be any help, now were they? No surprise really. He would just have to look into Teddy's death on his own then. Discreetly, of course. He could ask a few questions. Look into any opportunities that might have aided someone in killing Teddy Brewster. He would find a motive, if that's what Kelly wanted. JB still had several questions about the whole affair. For instance, when were the poppers slipped into Teddy's inhaler? And could those poppers have really killed him? Sure the fumes made the heart beat faster, but fast enough to kill? He'd have to check with a doctor about that. Who was Teddy's doctor? That's who he should start with.

◈ ◈ ◈

Doctor H. Kalpack's office was on the other side of Broadway facing Riverside Drive. The building was a WWII vintage four story of molded concrete and glass blocks. The doctor's lobby was crowded with people waiting for their appointments.

JB walked up to the nurse's station and inquired after the doctor. He even had a cover story all worked out. He would say he was working on a biography of Teddy's life. It gave him reason enough to be asking questions. And on the surface it was plausible. It could be checked out and would seem truthful to anyone who might inquire. Since he was a known writer the lie would make sense.

The nurse, an efficient sort, with a bun at the back of her neck and a set of little half glasses pinching her nose, said she would see if the doctor had time to speak with him. "Have a seat." She indicated the waiting room behind them.

He sat on a Danish wood frame and cord chair, held together by two thin foam cushions. Right out of the Nineteen-seventy's it still had it's nubby striped orange, yellow, and brown fabric on it. The doctor obviously wasn't concerned with decor. Nor with keeping up to date. That was clear from the Spring Nineteen-eighty *Good Housekeeping* magazine JB picked it up to read while he waited.

The nurse was back after two articles were read. JB now knew that menopause didn't need to be a trial if hormone drugs were prescribed and that Grace and Sam's (not their real names) marriage could be saved if only the couple would communicate with each other. The nurse leaned out her window and called his name, then had JB follow her. First behind her partition and then into a warren of exam rooms. She led him to one that was empty and left him to again wait. It was a good thing he had brought his magazine from the lobby, as the room was void of any reading material, save for a poster illustrating the food pyramid tacked on the wall beside the door.

Dr. Kalpack didn't keep JB waiting more than ten minuets. He knocked, backed in the room, then turned to face him. Looking like a double for Winston Churchill, minus the cigar, he inspected a chart he held in front of him.

"Now, what is it I can do for you today," he said, obviously mistaking JB for a patient. Then, right after, he said, "No, you wanted information for a book, didn't you. About Teddy Brewster, wasn't it?"

JB's writing a book about Teddy Brewster was looking to be a perfect cover. Human nature being what it is meant people love to talk about the famous they've had dealings with.

"That's right. I have Lee Arden's number if you would like to verify. She's the executor of his estate." JB wasn't a habitual liar, but he knew that details could make or break a fib.

The doctor looked him up and down. "No. It won't be necessary. What is it you want to know?"

"You were Teddy Brewster's physician for quite a long time. Right?"

The doctor nodded as he sat down heavily, setting the

loose skin hanging at his jaws aquiver.

"You even put together the bypass team that prolonged Teddy's life, didn't you? I'm thinking that you probably know quite a bit I can use in a book. I would give you source attribution, of course."

"All right. Let's see..." He wiped a hand across his mouth. "Mr. Brewster was a semi-healthy male in his early-fifties, with a history of heart and respiratory problems. The heart problem was what led to his demise. What else do you need to know?"

"I'm not really looking for medical factoids, Doctor. I can find that in his autopsy. What I do need is the more personal stuff. The human relations between doctor and patient. You knew him a long time. You must have been friends."

"No, I wouldn't say that. To be honest I knew him only as a patient. One visit a year for his annual checkup, and occasionally when he came down with something. But you want to know what kind of patient Teddy was, don't you?"

JB nodded. The doctor paused a moment to think to himself. Deciding if he should tell what he knew. He made his decision and began with...

"If you must know Teddy Brewster was possibly the worst patient I ever had the misfortune to acquire?" He crossed one leg over the other and folded his arms across his chest. "Yes, I can truthfully say Teddy Brewster might have been the devil incarnate. He was, in most regards, a terrible patient. A complete fool who would not listen to anything his medical team—that's team, with a capital T, mind you. That implies more than just me, Mr. Bent. There were other medical disciplines involved in his case. Well, he refused all of our advice and went on to actively pursue a completely hedonistic lifestyle. Do you know that while he was in hospital this last time he was cavorting in the rooms. He was having near orgies. He gambled with the orderly's. He never took his medications. There were even late night affairs with loose women. The floor nurses caught him pawing some woman several times."

" Yes, I'd heard that Teddy could be a handful."

"A truck load if you ask me."

"But you were his doctor long before his heart problems.

Isn't that right?"

"Yes. He first came to me because of a chronic problem with his breathing. We worked on that problem for several years."

"Then it was you that prescribed the menthol inhaler Teddy used to carry?"

"Why, yes." The doctor puffed up proud. "It was prescribed as a non-invasive, homeopathic approach to his breathing problems. As a dancer and an athlete, he needed to be able to breathe clearly. To have the nostrils open for air to get in. Together we came up with the remedy. The inhaler. It was really my grandmother's old-fashioned remedy. Teddy added the easy-carry inhaler."

"Is it possible that Teddy would have replaced the cotton inside the inhaler for an amulet of amyl-nitrite?"

The doctor nodded. The jowls rolled. They were like jello on springs. "It wouldn't surprise me. Teddy, defiantly, always did what he wanted. That meant everything that was against the rules of proper patient care. I was quite surprised when he demanded his release from the hospital. It was very quick and most unusual. But he had responded to his therapy so well. An example of the dancer as athlete..." Kalpack shook his head. The jowls made a soft slapping sound. "...so it was deemed appropriate for him to leave. Several more days in the hospital would have been beneficial I felt. I voiced my objections, but no one..."

Objections? The word caused JB to pay closer attention to what the doctor was saying.

"...would listen. A problem patient is quickly grown tired of by the staff. You know, the nurses actually run the wards, not the doctors. They're on the front lines, so to speak. Once they let it be known that they were tired of Teddy Brewster's antics, he was wheeled to the door and passed into his family's hands. He even did a dance step as he passed through the door. I had my doubts he would make it past the week if he returned to the stress he had been experiencing."

"Stress?"

"It's very fatiguing directing a Broadway show. That he survived less than a day was quite remarkable but not entirely unexpected."

"Would you have any idea why Teddy might be snorting inhalants directly after his surgery?"

"Inhalants, huh? Yes, I had heard that. That was the rumor that the ambulance boys passed around. They said he reeked of amyl when he was brought in. It wasn't prescribed for Teddy that was for sure. Gossip had it there was a woman. Amyl has been known to be used as a sexual aid, correct? And directly after leaving his hospital bed, mind you." He snorted. The jowls quivered again. "Teddy Brewster was always a randy little cuss."

And another legend was born—a tale to be passed around and gossiped about at cocktail parties all over Manhattan for years to come.

The story was that Teddy Brewster had killed himself using suicide by sex as his weapon of choice. The deceased wanted to go out "in the saddle" as the movie cowboys say. It would have made perfect sense to someone like Teddy. His entire life had been one long hedonistic indulgence. Teddy, with all the craziness, was forever in the midst of living life to the fullest. Getting the most from every day he was given. His heart problems were going to curtail that. If he had been thinking of suicide—and his deteriorating health could have led him to just that sort of thinking—who's to say he wasn't right?

JB, in thinking it through, realized Teddy might have been overwhelmed by the enormous effort that was expected of him in taking on the production of a Broadway musical. Even if theater was his life's blood, was it by the end too much to endure? Especially after the heart attacks. JB was also thinking it might have been those kind of thoughts that would cause a person with a weak heart to indulge in activities that would guarantee his demise. Further ruminating on the scant information that JB already had as witness to Teddy's death led him to an even more interesting conclusion. That if one had to fit sex—and the amyl certainly could lead one to that conclusion—into the time line of Teddy's last day the only person available for a tryst of the sort required would have had to be Lee Arden, his ex-wife.

Murder: Maybe?

It was clear to JB; and for that matter everyone else, Lee was still in love with the man, so having sex with him wouldn't be out of the question. That being the case, the sex would have been most likely from love and romance on her part, not for a pre-meditated murder. It didn't make sense that Lee Arden could be suspected of deliberately luring Teddy into having sex so he would die. I just didn't fit with her character, now did it?

Until she was hauled into the police station later that morning for questioning about what had suddenly become the murder of Teddy Brewster. She hadn't actually been arrested though. She was taken in only to give the cop's information about her involvement in what it was clear NYPD was now thinking might have been the assisted death of Teddy Brewster.

After JB had left Kelly's office the cop had mulled over JB's questions. Suppose he was right, Kelly started thinking? That it was the amyl that had killed Teddy Brewster? It couldn't hurt to check.

Kelly made a few phone calls doing some preliminary investigating. It took those few calls and he had found a good strong motive for what, to his mind, had now become a very suspicious death.

It turned out there was a two million dollar insurance policy on Teddy's life. That was motive galore for anyone. Teddy had his own personal insurance, beyond what the producers of *Mrs. MacKenzie's Muddle* had on him. What he had was a policy that would pay out big time for a natural death. It stipulated that such a death, as from a heart attack, would pay his beneficiary a two million payoff. And Lee Arden was the main beneficiary, along with Christopher getting a smaller share as Teddy's son.

Dance: Ten

Eleven

Never the type to give up on an idea that niggled at him, JB decided to have another talk with Jillian Morgan, the last mistress of Teddy Brewster.

Could she—maybe at one of the hospital room orgies Teddy reputedly had—have replaced the innards of his inhaler with amyl nitrite? She certainly had a good enough motive.

Jillian was a hometown ballet trained dancer until, new to New York, she had auditioned for Teddy Brewster. He offered her a place in his company, then soon elevated her to leads, and finally had offered her a golden apple in the guise of the part of Mrs. MacKenzie. But fate had stepped in and snatched it away when Betty Kane pulled out her contract and refused to relinquish the part. Jillian was, according to gossip, not at all angry with Betty for taking her part away. But she was livid with Teddy for caving in to Betty's demands. Revenge, in this case for a lost part, has been a good enough motive since Shakespeare was in business. And having a motive seemed to be the cops only need for arresting or questioning somebody on this case.

Look at Lee Arden. She had been taken to the precinct and questioned on what were the flimsiest of reasons. They had to let her go after—on JB's and Christopher's advice— Lee had lawyered up. But the police didn't do it without a warning that she was still a suspect. In what? Were the cops now considering Teddy Brewster's death suspicious? Well, join the party! JB was thinking.

JB made his way to Broadway then up to Times Square, purported in song to be "naughty, bawdy, gaudy, and sporty". With its twenty-four hour grind triple-X movie theater's and raw sex peep shows, the area really was more crummy, scummy, bummy, and slummy. JB had to run that gauntlet to get to the Zigfield Theater, where rehearsals for *Mrs. MacKenzie's Muddle* were then in progress.

Once inside the theater he spotted Jillian Morgan standing at the back of the house. After reminding her where they had met previously he asked her to meet with him out in the lobby.

JB waited a few minutes. She soon joined him.

She was more than willing to talk with JB. She was, in fact, almost desperate to rid herself of some the angst and worry she had been holding on to. She was quickly in tears and relaying her most secret fears to JB. As if he was her therapist or a trusted confidant. It all poured out in a rush, washing over both of them, leaving them both exhausted and drained

JB decided, on their second meeting, that she really wasn't the calculating, ambitious, and clutching actress she was being portrayed as by the gossips. More Mary Sunshine than Eve Harrington. JB was finding her rather sweet and earnest, if not a bit naive. Dancing and Teddy Brewster were the two things that had filled her life for the last year or so. With Teddy's death she now found herself in a quandary. How would she fill the void?

She really had loved Teddy, JB decided. And she did have every right to be this upset. She had been Teddy's favorite, and had for a brief moment achieved every dance gypsies dream. To be pulled from the chorus and made a star. Little Jillian Morgan, who took up dance because her mother thought her gawky, had been cast as the lead in a Teddy Brewster production. True, it was only a revival, but it had bones, and would have been noticed.

Then that lead part was rudely pulled away from her at the last minute. "By that crone that had done the show eons before," Jillian pouted. She went on to tell JB that Betty Kane had demanded that she be kept in the lead. "The bitch used her contract and her clout to have me fired. And then Betty stood there gloating while Teddy told me. In front of everybody. It was so embarrassing. Teddy had never treated me like that before."

JB nodded, having heard most of what had happened from Len, which he had picked up from the gossips swirling around in the company. "That scene hurt me as a professional, Mr. Bent. Mrs. MacKenzie as Teddy was making it for me was a career part."

What had made it even more awkward was everyone knew Jillian had been sleeping with Teddy. It was thought by those in the cast she had done that to get considered for the part in the first place. And that was the reason for much of the negative gossip about her.

But what JB was hearing through her sobs was that she was as surprised as anyone else that she was given the part. True, it had been her listening to Teddy's pillow talk that had led him to come up with the idea of a younger more sex-charged Mrs. MacKenzie. But she never expected him to cast her in the role. Then, she was saying, she considered herself lucky when she had been hired to work on the dance numbers of what was now Christopher's show. It was like she was rising like a firebird. Currently the dance director on *Mrs. MacKenzie's Muddle* it was actually providing her with a new career direction.

Completely disarmed by the woman JB had let her ramble. Now he zeroed in on his most pressing question. He asked, "I know this is personal, Jillian, but did Teddy use poppers when you were together?"

She lit a cigarette, then nodded. "It made it better for him. I didn't like them so much."

"So, he would have kept his amyl nitrite capsules there in the apartment you shared?"

"They were around. In the bedside table mostly."

"So anyone who was there in the apartment would have had access to them."

"If they were in the bedroom for some reason."

"Who were your visitors right before and after Teddy had his first heart attack?"

"God, after the attack everybody was in and out of the place. Getting things he needed at the hospital. Packing clothes. All sorts of people. Lee was there. His lawyer. The producer on *Mrs. MacKenzie*. Gofers from the show. Everybody was in and out. Even a bunch of the guys from the chorus came by. They tried to make me feel better."

So, JB was thinking, it could have been anyone that had taken a capsule of amyl and then used it to kill Teddy. JB decided that Jillian's lack of disappointment over losing that part most likely wouldn't have made her want to kill the man who had taken the part away from her? That put her at bottom place on his list of suspects. Jillian, who should have been angry enough to kill, had instead accepted what opportunity had come along and found in it a new direction. She wasn't a murderer. JB didn't think vengeance was a word that even had a place in her vocabulary.

"Then Teddy had to go and die," she was saying. "Totally killing any chance of keeping the vision we were both aiming for. Teddy, you see, was thinking in the realm of a dance opera. He wanted the entire show told with movement. It would have been spectacular, Mr. Bent. He knew his heart was weak. He told me he wanted the last show he directed to be the show he had dreamed of creating since he'd worked in Hollywood as a hoofer back in the fifties. Not a bunch of different musical selections that most dance recitals are, but telling a real story. With movement. He said he was aiming for what Fred Astaire was doing in his movies. Teddy even made me watch *The Ziegfeld Follies* just for the 'Limehouse Blues' number. He was aiming to make his production of *Mrs. MacKenzie's Muddle* a landmark show in musical theater history." Jillian dabbed at her eyes with a wad of tissue she found tucked in her bosom. "I'm sorry, I didn't mean to get so emotional. But when I think of what might have been."

"Yet, you've stayed with the production. From what you said, you've even started a new career."

Jillian looked at him. "Huh?"

"As an interpreter of Teddy Brewster's dance style. You could be the one to keep his particular style alive, Jillian. Like the Glenn Miller Band is still together, and plays music in the orchestral arrangements that Miller invented. They've kept his music alive. You can do the same with Teddy's work. Teaching the Brewster style to a new generation of dancers."

Then who's next?, JB was thinking. Who else might have had reason to want Teddy Brewster dead? JB decided to visit the rooftop rehearsal room to work out the next step. He now had a reason to attend what were usually closed rehearsals. He was a member of the crew. Christopher had actually hired him to do the rewrites on the libretto, which meant JB sitting in the stalls and watching a rehearsal was a natural event. Besides, it also gave JB and Christopher opportunities to get together for a fast grab and tickle when the oppertunity presented itself. The theater bathrooms were perfect for a quick assignation. They had even found one with a lock.

Dance: Ten

Twelve

Christopher
and JB were huddled side by side in the fifth row of seat's in
the old rooftop theater of the Zigfield Theater right smack
dab in the middle of New York City and Times Square.
Right there on the fabled Broadway. Originally the space
had been used for the *Nighttime Frolics* in the nineteen-
twenty's. Now it was being used because it had a small
stage on which to rehearse. JB took a moment to savor the
feeling. To be in the same historic theater where the likes of
Fanny Brice and Will Rodgers had performed. Not so shabby
for an escapee from nowhere Kansas to have accomplished.
Mixing with the hoi-palooy as his mother would put it.

The two men had a brief conversation, then Christopher
stood and turned toward his actors. They were standing on

the stage at the front. Christopher spoke loudly. "Could we run act one, scene three, please. The lead in to the song. Thank you."

He sat back down.

Len Matthews as Mr. Van Roddy and Lee Arden as Mrs. MacKenzie took their places and readied themselves to begin. They paused; waiting for a go ahead.

Without standing, simply making a gesture, Christopher said, "Sorry, go ahead." Then he leaned to JB, "This is one of the scenes I was wondering about. It doesn't come off funny, and it should."

JB pulled his knees up, "Let me watch," and focused his attention on the actors.

> *Mrs. MacKenzie: Do you sleep as nature intended?*
> *Mr. VanRoddy: I've done nothing as nature intended.*

"Its a matter of rhythm, Christopher. If he says the line as *I've never done anything as nature intended*, it should get you a laugh."

Christopher left JB sitting where he was and went up on the stage to speak with his actors.

JB made a note of the change and then sat a moment. He looked around the theater. The seating area he was in wasn't lit; only the stage lights were being used. The little theater with seating for a mere two hundred had pockets of light where the tarnished gold filigree sconces along the walls were turned down to dim. JB saw Ronald Prescott, the producer of the show, behind him, sitting in one of the light pools over on the side. He was sifting through a leather portfolio of mail. Reading a letter, making a note on it, then restoring it to its envelope.

JB stood and went over to talk with him. He slid along the seats until he was standing next to him. "Mr. Prescott, I just wanted to thank you for bringing me on as a writer today. It will be a nice credit."

Ronald turned in his seat to face JB. "You won't be credited. I thought that was understood."

"Yes, yes, of course I knew. I just meant the word might get around within the community. I can always use the fees that show-doctoring make." JB chuckled.

"Christopher wanted you. As long as he's happy."

"He's kind of coming to your rescue isn't he? And you'll still be getting a Teddy Brewster production even with him dying. You'll make a fortune out of this show. I'm sure of it." JB sat down next to the producer. "With this cast and now Christopher stepping in as director I think you have a sure fire two or three year run here. On the cast alone it'll run a year. Until their contracts run out."

Ronald grinned. "True. Christopher's coming on board is going to save the production. And he's much easier to get along with. Teddy, for some reason, was becoming impossible. He had never been like that before. But, he had this vision for this particular show. It was going to be a totally different play that what had been done previously. To be honest, Bent, it would have ruined me. Dance opera, my foot."

"Call me JB. Everyone does. Then you're not going to miss Teddy as your director then? He was that difficult to work with?"

"At the end? Yes. Quite frankly, I was afraid that Teddy was going to bankrupt me. If we had gone on with his ideas and it flopped, which I can assure it would have." He shuttered. "I would have had to return all the investors deposits. This show is financed in the millions. You know, musicals have become so damn expensive to produce. From now on I do only plays. What I want is a nice quiet five character, one set, easy-peasy, production."

JB had started out trying to glean something from Ronald Prescott. Now here was their conversation turning into a pitch meeting. Oh well, JB figured, it would probably be to his advantage to go with the flow.

"We should discuss that Mr. Prescott." JB loathed selling himself. That's why he paid an agent. However, it became necessary when said agent wasn't around to do it for him.

"I've had a play on Broadway myself. I might be interested in writing another."

"Would you? Yes, that's something to discuss. Get in touch with me after you finish here."

He turned back to his mail.

JB took the hint and returned to his seat down front.

◆◆◆

Len stood one row down and directly in front of JB, who was again slouched in his seat in the fifth row.

"I should have known it was your fine hand stirring up this little cauldron of dialogue. *Always*? Really? Since when do *you* give *me* line readings?"

"Its the song of the sentence, Len."

"Is that the same as the *rhythm*?" The sarcasm dripped like candle wax.

"Christopher told you that, did he? Well, that's just what I mean."

Len shrugged.

"Did you hear the emphasis you just now used on the word *rhythm*?" JB said it back to Len, imitating him. "Think of it as a line in a song, Len. You could even call it a pre-song solo for you. It is that musical. "

Len looked at him, doubtful but interested.

"If you think of the line as being a beat for every word. *Anything* is a sort of hiccup. They're the lines being used as the lead-in to a song, Len. Its okay to start the ball rolling. Think of the opening in *Music Man*."

"You did say solo?" Len considered a moment. "You think I could get away with it?"

JB nodded.

"Okay. I can give it a try."

"Great. Now, can I ask you to shift over just a teence." JB's hand made a fish swimming gesture. "I want to watch Lee."

As Len stepped to the side, he asked, "What's a *teence*?"

"A couple of steps on the way to teensy-tiny."

"O-K-a-a-y" Len gave him one of those *have you gone nuts* looks but he sat.

"I'm absolutely amazed at her." JB indicated Lee delivering her lines on stage. "After what she went through this morning and she's still standing. I probably would have fainted from nervous exhaustion and taken to my bed."

"Who should have fainted?" Len asked. "You don't mean Lee? What happened? She hasn't said *anything*." Len was trying out his hiccup. He shook his head no. Then Len looked again at JB. "Although, she was late for rehearsal

92

today, and Christopher took her to task. But he had just got here himself, so he had no right to be miffed with her. What I don't understand is that so far he's been a dream director. This entire rehearsal period has been such a joy. I don't even care if we open. The rehearsal money is plenty good enough just for the experience of working on the show. But, if you tell anyone I said that I'll have your nads for breakfast."

"Colorful, Len. And not altogether appetizing."

"You don't have them for the flavor. Its for the vengence. Sometimes you are so dense."

JB shrugged. "What's not to see?"

There was a rumpus on stage as a member of the crew was bringing a cafe chair out from the wings for the now prostrate leading lady. Lee had suddenly collapsed, and was hanging like washday laundry onto Christopher's shoulders. His arms were wrapped around her to help hold her up. The chair was set next to them and Christopher bent to sit his mother in it.

Out in the stalls JB half rose from his seat.

"I was afraid of something like this."

Len, now also standing, said, "What's happened?"

They listened as Lee's voice rang out in the little space. She was protesting to Christopher that there was no need for her to have medical attention and agreed to go on to the end of the scene. She tried standing, and immediantly sunk back onto the chair. She looked up at her son, "You know, darling, perhaps an hour in my dressing room would be helpful."

Christopher began to walk her off stage. At the wings he stopped and called a break, then again began to help his mother to her dressing room.

Len turned back to JB.

"Now what exactly was it you were saying about this morning? Start with what's going on with Lee?"

"This is strictly between you and me, Len. Nads included." JB grabbed his crotch.

"Charming," Len said. "And so graphicly picaresque."

"It's meant to emphasize my point." JB leaned forward in his seat. "This can't get out, Len. You mustn't tell anyone."

Dance: Ten

Len said, "All right, already. I get it."

JB looked from side to side to make sure they wouldn't be overheard. "Lee was taken by the police to the station this morning for questioning in the now possibly suspicious circumstances of Teddy Brewster's death."

Len gave an appropriate response—an intake of breath. "You mean they think it was murder?" he said.

JB went on. "I told you there might be more to this than suicide, didn't I? Christopher and I were at the police station to get her released this morning. I waited there with her while her lawyer and Christopher got the details worked out."

That had been the least of it.

Lieutenant Kelly was being his usual obstinate self, holding them up in the hallway.

Christopher and JB had, that morning, been cozily lying together when Lee had called. The answering machine picked up. Her panicked voice had got them both sitting up immediantly. They were dressed and at the precinct station in less than twenty minutes.

Lieutenant Kelly was now intent on keeping them from getting to her. Kelly's bushy eyebrows scrunched together on his brow like two caterpillars having sex. He was thinking about an answer to Christopher's frantic concerns dealing with his mother.

"Why, in God's name, are you holding her?" Christopher demanded.

The Lieutenant growled his answer. "This is your fault, Bent. Blame him for Miss Arden being questioned." Kelly crossed his arms. A bulwark blocking their path.

"What?" JB asked incredulously. "How is this my fault?"

Christopher, standing next to JB, looked sideways at him. "You started this?"

"How could I?" It's ridic..." JB turned back to Kelly. "You mean from my talk with you the other day?"

Kelly answered with a nod.

"Come on, Kelly. From a possible suicide to murder? And Lee Arden as your suspect? That's a real reach. You said to find you solid evidence. What possible reason was there for Lee Arden to kill her ex-husband. Hell, she slept with him an hour before he died."

Christopher backed up and sat heavily on a line of molded plastic chairs against the wall. JB turned to him.

"Oh dear, you didn't know about Lee and Teddy sleeping together that last morning? You must have joined the party after they left the hospital. Was that at his apartment."

Christopher nodded.

"I had breakfast and then joined them at Teddy's. He wanted to change from what he was wearing at the hospital. When I got there he was insisting on going to the rehearsal. To bolster the troops as he put it. I was only in and out of the apartment that morning."

JB said, "You know that there's been some gossip about Teddy using sex as a weapon to kill himself. I know that's blunt but we don't have much time for niceties. This is becoming very serious. I know you must have heard the rumors..."

Christopher shook his head. "I haven't heard anything about that. What does it have to do with this situtition?"

".Well, it means that the .only person who was accessible as a partner for him between the hospital and his place that morning was Lee. His ex-wife."

Christopher snorted. "You don't know Teddy. He could have managed an orgy with the Radio City Rockettes in that amount of time."

JB smiled. That was Teddy's reputation again. JB didn't think Lee would have participated in that sort of scene. She just didn't seem the bacchanalian type. Although, it did mean Christopher Brewster's being at the apartment would add him to JB's list of people with opportunity for murder. He was one more on an ever lengthening list of the people who were in and out of Teddy's place.

"We found another reason," Kelly grunted, the eyebrows now raised and separated. "A two-million dollar reason."

"What are you talking about?"

Christopher stood. "It must be Teddy's insurance policy. That was a publicity stunt, Lieutenant. Teddy was working on a movie script about the insurance industry. He took out the policy to get newspaper space for his project."

"Yet he kept up the payments every month. And made you and Miss Arden beneficiaries."

JB said, "If that's all it takes then why don't you question Christopher?"

Kelly rocked back and forth. Then indicated a cop standing behind them. JB and Christopher turned. Christopher looked back.

"You want to question me too?"

"I'm afraid so. Would you go with the officer?"

The cop escorted him down the hallway.

"Bent, you'll get in to see Miss Arden when we finish with her."

"Then I'm calling her lawyer right now."

He started to follow Christopher and the cop.

"Christopher. Who do I call?"

"Well, the lawyer got them both out of there within the hour," JB finished telling Len. "Isn't it interesting though? The police now think that a motive is all you need to haul someone in. That idiotic idea was what led them to Lee. There's a large insurance policy on Teddy, hence she had a motive for killing him. In my book, opportunity and nature are far more reliable deciding factors. Is the person your looking at capable of the crime?" JB spread out his arms. "Look at the woman, Len. How could anyone think Lee Arden would kill someone?"

Len scratched his head. "Anyone can kill, JB. There are no restrictions on who might murder. But I will have to agree with you. Lee is the least likely person I know to have killed anyone."

He sat silently a moment, then turned back to JB.

"But I have to ask. Isn't that the same defense that got Lizzie Borden a not guilty verdict? The thinking was that she was too much of a lady to have axed her mother and father to death? At least that's what the papers of the time reported."

"The newspapers? That's why there's a veil of secrecy on this, Len."

"You've got to be kidding. A veil! Who are you? Victor Hugo?"

"With a threat of castration remember. No, Len, the

Murder: Maybe?

sort of publicity this could generate would hurt Lee. And the show too. So far we've been safe. The tabloid guys don't have it yet. The show's publicity people are going to spin it so more isn't made out of it than is necessary. On Lee's insistence, by the way. She's been on tabloid front pages before. Back when she and Teddy divorced."

"Something we have in common," Len said dryly. He was thinking back to his drinking days and his own stories in the pages of the rags. "But you know what? I find it very interesting that you even have a place in all this, JB. I didn't know you and Christopher were so close."

JB was thinking, Oh. Oh. There goes Len sniffing down the wrong pathway again. Bloodhounds weren';t as persistant. JB needed to re-direct the way Len was heading. And fast. He leaned forward and put his hands on the back of the seat in front of him.

"Close? I wouldn't say we were all that close. I've been hired as a writer to work on the original script. To modernize it and bring it more in line with Christopher's vision for the production. The libretto is from the sixties, you know? Things have changed. Jokes get creaky. Rhythms, if you will?"

JB leaned over and mock slugged Len on the shoulder. JB watched Len, to see if his sleight of hand conversation, his conjuring trick of misdirection, had worked.

"So what's next on your agenda?" Len asked.

My God, JB sighed to himself. He's let it pass. There is magic in the world.

"I want to talk to the people who were at that last rehearsal meeting of Teddy's. You know, Len, right before we ran into them on Columbus Avenue. Lee mentioned it."

Len nodded. "That would have included the entire cast then. And, let's see, Ronald Prescott as well. And the dance chorus. And, oh yes, the dance accompanist probably was in the room too."

"Then I have a gang of people to talk to, don't I."

97

Dance: Ten

Thirteen

Finding
the cast turned out not to be such a hard thing to do after all.
Len had to return to his own rehearsal, so JB went to stand
alone in the front lobby of the quiet theater. He listened,
then aimed for where he heard a piano playing.

That led him to a mirrored rehearsal hall on the
mezzanine level of the theater. There the chorus was going
through one of the dance numbers as Jillian Morgan clapped
and kept count for them. It looked like the rehearsed number
was only using the women. There was a row of men sitting
or standing in various attitudes around the perimeter of the
room. The piano was pounding out the tune raucously while
the dancers went through their paces.

Standing in a corner leaning against the wall JB spotted

the man he and Len had talked with that day at Lee's place. At Teddy's wake. The man with the gossipy nature.

JB, knowing he could use that exact trait, went over to him and said, "Hey. I don't know if you remember me?"

The man looked at JB.

"Sure. Your Len's friend. You were at Lee Arden's with him. A couple of weeks ago," and he giggled.

Giggled? About a wake?

"That's right."

"What can I do for you?"

"Well, since then I've started working on a book about Teddy. I write you know?" The man indicated he did. "I was wondering if we could talk. You might have some insights into his personality that would be useful."

The guy nodded, then held a finger to his lips. He pointed over to the moving dancers. He reached down, picked up his bag, and indicated JB should follow him. They left the rehearsal room and stood together in the hall. JB noticed, as close as they were, that he dyed his hair. A chestnut color. He was riding quickly into middle age too He must have been a stunner when younger. The kid every queen wanted. Age, however wasn't being so kind. Sallow skin, bags beginning to form under the eyes, scalp showing through thinning hair. Because of his profession, JB supposed, he did still have a tight muscular body.

"Sorry," he said. "I don't want to disturb Jillian while she's working. Now, what was it you wanted?"

"As I said, I'm working on a book about Teddy. Can we talk?", JB asked quoting Joan Rivers.

The book gambit had worked with the doctor maybe it would go over here too?

"I was wondering about the last time you saw Teddy. It was at the meeting right after he got out of the hospital, right?"

There was a slight glare of suspicion in the corner of the man's eye. Oops, too quick to the point JB realized.

"But, first, tell me something about you. Your life as a dancer."

His expression changed to a smile. Suspicion erased. Ego wining once again.

"Well, my name isn't really Jimmy Jameson. When I

went to Equity there was already an Arthur Jameson..."

When an actor signs with the union if another person already has your name you have to find another. Thus Joe Lane becomes Nathan Lane, his favorite character in *Guys And Dolls*. And Arthur obviously became Jimmy.

"...My father's name was James. I became Jimmy Jameson right then and there. And I've been dancing ever since. Twenty years now. With only a little break a few years ago. I tried opening my own studio. That went bust, so I came back to New York to work. The best it's ever been was getting in with Teddy..."

JB wasn't really listening. His mind had started wondering; worrying over that earlier giggle of Jimmy's. What was that about? It was at the mention of Len, wasn't it? You don't suppose that the two of them? No, Len wasn't usually susceptible to chorus boy's charms. He went for a tougher variety of man. Construction workers, gym bunnies. Then again, earlier Len had let JB's connection with Christopher get by him hadn't he? That was odd. Not at all like Len to let a hint of *la affaire de intrigue* get past him. What would explain that? Maybe that he's preoccupied with his own affairette at the moment? That would explain...

Jimmy was winding up his story.

"...So, this will be my last show. I'm thirty-eight." JB figured forty. "Too long in the tooth to still be dancing eight shows a week. It's hard on the body parts, you know? There isn't enough *Ben-Gay* in all of Manhattan to help anymore."

"I'll bet," JB said. "So how did most of the dancers feel about Teddy?"

"Teddy was our guru. Our swami. The chief. Any of us would have followed him anywhere. There isn't a gypsy on Broadway that didn't want to work with him. He was a genius. A bit tortured maybe, and self-destructive, as we all can be, but what a force he was."

"Self-destructive?"

"Smoking for one thing. That cigarette always on his lip. Couldn't have been good for him. He was a dancer, for crips sake."

"What about the inhaler?"

"That too. We all thought there was some illegal

something in that thing. When he was stumped for a move in a routine he would take a snort off it. Then he'd come up with something brilliant. It was magic, I tell you."

JB was taken aback. Hadn't he just been thinking about magic? Guess we all have to find our own brand of magic. Pills, B-12 injections. Whatever. Teddy's was in an inhaler. JB used writing as his prestidigitational fix. Everyone needs their tricks in varying doses.

"Even at that last meeting?"

"There too. In fact, there was a bit of a hubbub over it that day. He couldn't find it and there was a rush of people to look for it."

That's it, JB snapped to himself. That's when the menthol had to have been switched for the amyl. From then on that inhaler was a lethal weapon. Just waiting to take its victim at the next snort. To virtually breathe death.

"Who did? Find the inhaler, I mean?"

Jimmy thought a moment. "You know I don't remember. But it was found and they got it back to him."

"How was Teddy that day? Did he seem ill?"

"Well, he was weak. Lee had to hold him up when he came in. They were draped all over each other. And he was pale. All of us were surprised he was even there. It had only been a week or so since he'd had his surgery. He should have still been in the hospital. But, there he was. Trying for his usual boisterous self. It was an act, of course. But we all went along with it."

"Morale boosting was he?"

"Right. We all wanted him to be well, so we kind of overlooked his real condition. That's the worst of it. None of us got a chance to tell him how much we cared. He didn't know how we all thought of him."

"I'm sure he did, Jimmy. On some level he had to know that he was loved by all of you. What if you all did this show so it would stand as a memorial to him. That would please him, don't you think?"

"Maybe." He reached for his bag. "If that's true then I'd better get in there and rehearse. We open for previews in less than a month."

"Well, thanks, Jimmy. You've been very helpful."

"Glad to. If you need more just ask."

"I thought you said you were leaving the show..."

"To go into antiques. Sure, but a steady job on Broadway can pay for a lot of Chippendale tables. I'll be here for the foreseeable future."

Jimmy headed back to the hall.

"If you need me just let Len know. He'll pass on the word on to me."

Just let Len know? That's telling, JB thought. Maybe there really is something going on there. Between those two. Well, good. It would take Len's attention away and keep it out of JB's business.

Dance: Ten

Fourteen

◆◆◆◆◆◆◆◆◆◆◆◆◆◆◆◆Jimmy
went back into the rehearsal room followed closely by JB.
But JB stopped at the door for a look around first.

Who was he going to talk to next? Jillian was in the
midst of a discussion with the cast. All of them were crowded
around her to listen. Over at the piano the rehearsal
pianist sat making a notation on his sheet music. There
were probably thirty people in the rehearsal room. Who did
he need to talk with? Were any or all of them at that last
meeting? Needles in stacks, anyone?

Plays, JB had found, were much easier to keep track of
the basic personnel. A producer, director, actors, writer and
the crew. Boom. Easy. A musical, on the other hand, was
nearly impossible. Cast and crew could number as many as
sixty or seventy people. Count the orchestra and you're up
in the hundreds. In the music department alone there were
usually a team of writers—lyricist and composer (unless

they were the same person), then there was the music orchestrator, vocal arranger, orchestra conductor, dance and vocal accompanists, dance director and assistants, and on and on. All under the charge of the music director.

That last meeting with Teddy, JB realized, could have had any one of maybe ten different people from the music department alone working with the cast that day. Hell, with this revival of *Mrs. MacKenzie's Muddle* they had even gone back to the original composer—well, actually his wife, since he had died five year's ago—and found a song that had been eliminated from the show right before opening twenty years before. She had found the sheet music among his effects and was allowing them to use it as a new number for this production. Even she could have been at the meeting. JB figured the pianist was as good a person as any to talk with first. Len had said the accompanist would have been there. Maybe he could give JB a clue.

It turned out he was known to JB. The local cable company in New York had a public access channel in its line-up. Anyone who wanted to produce their own TV show could use the company's facilities and broadcast over their airwaves. There were drag queens, porn stars, political extremists, and Harold Wallenwitz. All with their own shows.

Harold was on public access TV every Friday at 9PM. It wasn't much of a show. It consisted of him sitting at a piano telling show-biz stories and gushing over his favorite songwriters. He was crazy for Jerry Herman. As it turned out, Harold was also the accompanist on *Mrs. MacKenzie*.

Harold was a tall thin man somewhere in his fifties, with a tortured lavender colored hair style that started a half inch above his right ear, went straight up, then swooped into a dip onto his forehead and circled to cover the bald spot lurking at the back of his head. He wore large blue plastic framed glasses that made his face seem as if it was peering out from under a microscope.

JB sat next to him and asked point blank if he had been at that last meeting.

He had, so using the same ego smoothing opening JB used with Jimmy Jameson he soon was able to get him talking. "What can you tell me about Teddy Brewster?"

He snorted. "Then may I be blunt?"

"I hope you will be. I'm looking for people to tell me their honest feelings about the man,"

"Well then, Teddy Brewster, contrary to many peoples opinions, was basicily a Bob Fosse imitator."

Wallenwitz's voice was similar to Noel Cowards; snide, condescending, and wrapped in ermine.

"If you asked Teddy he was the love child of a midnight romp between Jerome Robbins and Agnes de Mille. What he actually was was a so-so dancer who pushed the modicum of talent he had to its outer reaches."

The pianist didn't come off quite so waspish on TV. Another example of the *Gerber*-rization of television itself. It presented to the public only what would save a network from a libel suit.

"But if you tell Lee Arden I said that I'll deny it. You know how she is? To her Teddy was Terpsichore the Muse of Dance. Maybe he was to some. I found him loud and tedious. A tambourine will only carry you so far."

"You weren't a fan then?"

"His work was always derivative. He stole from Fosse, Bennett, Tharp, Robbins, old forties movies. He even stole from himself. Recycling steps from previous shows ad infinitum."

"What was your impression on that last day?" This should be interesting JB thought. "How was he looking?"

"He was ringing the bell of death's door. And death was willing to answer. He looked terrible. I have no idea why he was here. Unless the rumors were true, and they were looking for a replacement."

"They?"

"The producers, of course."

"Really? What can you tell me about the inhaler incident? Did you see that?"

"Sure. It was Teddy being a diva again. Much to-do over very little. He had left the thing in his coat pocket. It was retrieved and handed over to him."

"And who did that?"

"Who? Let me think....Someone in the cast, I suppose. No, that wasn't it." Wallenwitz thought for a moment, then grinned. "Oh, yes, of course, it was Ronald. Ronald

Prescott."

And the cell door clanged closed. If that moment was the moment the switch was made, as JB suspected, then Ronald had to be the killer. Ronald? The producer of *Mrs. MacKenzie's Muddle* was the murderer? There was a reason, of course. Ronald had said so himself. He would have been bankrupt if Teddy had made a flop out of the show. And according to all the scuttlebutt that was just what was happening. Lieutenant Kelly wanted motive. JB had a doozey for him.

◆◆◆

JB spent the rest of the day talking with the other members of the cast from Teddy's last meeting. He didn't glean much that would have been useful even if the book he said he was writing was a reality. The dancers were all acolytes and members of the Teddy cult that had always surrounded him when he was alive. What JB got was outright fawning and gushingly worshipful comments about the man. Especially now that he was dead.

The only thing useful anyone said was one person mentioning that Teddy and Ronald Prescott had been partners and friends for a very long time. JB hadn't realized their relationship went back to before even Teddy and Lee had first met. And it is a fact that killers were often well known to their victims. The cell door key was turning for Prescott as the evidence was piling up against him.

JB didn't put much stock in the complimentary remarks made on Teddy's behalf. JB knew better than to believe the majority of it. Broadway gossip had it, before his death, that Teddy was demanding, perverse, and could be vindictive. Never forgetting any slight or snub. Or a bad review. It was discovered that Teddy carried a creased and yellowed copy of the first bad review he had ever receive (back in the fifties) in his wallet. And the critic that had written it was still banned from seeing or reviewing any of Teddy's shows. That's holding a grudge. Now that he was gone, however, Teddy would be in the process of having his reputation redeemed.

All the great or famous went through the same process. That's why Cole Porter wasn't gay, and J. Edgar Hoover wasn't a transvestite. The shortcomings and peccadilloes of the famous were conveniently swept into the background to be whispered about at dinner and cocktail parties. Perhaps any book on the real Teddy Brewster would have to wait for the softening of time.

Dance: Ten

ifteen

Len and JB hadn't been able to hook up for quite some time since both were knee-deep in rehearsals. Both were busy much of the time so all they had been able to manage was hurried conversations when they met in the theater on the way to a meeting or a cast call. *Hi, How are you?. Fine. Good. Gotta run*, wasn't satisfactory to JB's way of thinking. The remedy JB decided was to stop at the local *Gristidie's* and pick up the ingredients for his famous mock chicken curry. Len could be enticed by it to come down for a meal over rice that evening.

JB dipped a wooden spoon into the simmering sauce and holding his hand under it made his way up to Len's apartment door. When Len answered his knock he held out the spoon. "Taste this. Does it need something?"

Len leaned forward, and stuck out his tongue. "Um. Curry?" He smacked his lips. "Maybe a touch more cumin?"

"Right. How about coming down for dinner?"

"I love it when you go all Betty Crocker. Give me a minute." Len turned and disappeared into his living room.

JB shouted after him. "Couldn't you at least give me a manly cook. How about *The Galloping Gourmet?*"

Len came back to the door. As he slipped into a sweater, he said, "More like *The Prancing Provender*, I'd say."

They went down the stairs to JB's apartment.

JB used a piece of bread and scraped up the last of the sauce on his plate. Len leaned back in his chair.

"This was such a good idea, JB. I've been meaning to talk to you."

"What's on your mind, Len?"

"About the rewrite you've been doing on *Mrs. MacKenzie.*"

"What about it? Its coming along very nicely, if I do say so myself. At least, Christopher seems to be pleased."

"But what I want to know is are you being too radical? That added scene with the principals? Its funny, sure, but maybe its too farcical for the show? This isn't funny things happening at forums, you know."

Len was referring to the newly discovered song they had found in a trunk with the composer's widow. It had been incorporated and was being used as a quartet between the two couples. Len and Lee and Betty and Jerry. It included a late night mix-up of beds and partners that rose quickly to outlandish absurdity.

"You have to admit it's totally different in tone to the rest of the show, JB. There's a charm in *Mrs. MacKenzie* that seems lost in all the raucousness of this new number. That's what got Teddy in trouble, remember? Do we really need to follow in his footsteps."

"Hum, you may be right. I'll tell you what, I'll bring it up with Christopher next time I see him. Although, so far he's been supportive of the concept. In any event, we'll know better once previews start next week, right? If it is too out there it can be toned down, or even eliminated. The audience always tells us what works and what doesn't. But for now I'll do what Christopher asks me to do. We aim in his direction."

"Is that true when you two are at home together too?"

JB stiffened. "What are you talking about?"

"Oh pooh, JB. You think I haven't guessed that you and Christopher are getting it on? I'm not the right type for him, my ass? You just wanted him all for yourself. I'll have you know I am much more of a smart-ass than a dumb-ass, so of course, I caught on to you two stealing off for moments together. For weeks now. It was like watching something Joe Orton wrote. *What The Co-star Saw.* Practically slobbering all over each other in the bathrooms. Really, JB, very high school."

"And what about you and Jimmy Jameson? For your information I had that figured out too. You've hid nothing. At least from me."

"I should have known. You read way too much Agatha Christie. Finding clues in the innocuous. What tipped it?"

"Jimmy said something when we talked. He didn't do it on purpose, but he told me."

"Okay, so you and I are both seeing somebody. Is it serious with you and Christopher?"

"Serious? I wouldn't call it that. He's certainly a sexy beast, and we are hot for each other. I'm beginning to suspect it's purely lust though. We do want each other. All the time. But I don't see anything serious coming out of it. I mean, he isn't even out of the closet."

"And that bothers you?"

"Of course it does, but, Len, he's got to be one of the best lays I've had in years. I even get hard just thinking about it. What about you?"

"I seldom erect at maudlin fairytales of lust and overwrought gonads."

JB hurumped. "That's not what I meant."

"Oh, then you mean Jimmy? Actually, I am quite fond of him, but I wouldn't say it will have any lasting impact. The sex is non-existent. We did it once and then never seemed to get around to it again. Mostly, I'm thinking of helping him in his antique business. As an investment. He's really very astute in the field. Did I tell you about the cane?"

"Cane?"

"Do you remember the cane I used in *The Greenhouse Murders?*" Len went on to explain that Jimmy had found out it was valuable, and that it just went to show how good Jimmy would be as a dealer. So Len was contemplating lending him startup money for his shop.

"Len, what are you thinking? You can't seriously be giving money to an almost complete stranger. You've only known him for a few weeks. I would question his character before I go giving away cash money."

"What are you saying?"

"Len, Jimmy is, from my observation, just about everything you've said you hate about show business. He's a gossipy chorus boy. He's a great big queen. Although he is very good looking. But, he's been a Broadway gypsy for how many years? Twenty? And in all that time he hasn't saved enough to finance his own business? That seems very irresponsible. If you invest in him what makes you think you'll get your money back? You need to put your cash into something that will pay you a dividend. The market maybe?"

"I'm not sure, but isn't all of that the definition of investment? Taking a gamble? Your saying my money would be better off put in the stock market? Of which I know absolutely nothing. I do, however have some knowledge of antiques and collectibles."

"With Jimmy being a collectible? Don't your AA friends call that taking a hostage."

"You do have a perverse way of thinking. At least Jimmy's close to my own age. What is it with you and bringing home these lost boys of yours? They're not like puppies, JB. You can't just paper train them and forget them. I just don't get the younger man thing? First there was that affairette with Toby, now this child."

JB was tempted to answer by breaking into a chorus of the old song *They Make Me Feel So Young*. And to extend the metaphor, they also made him feel desirable. And alive. Gay men, JB was well aware of, have a lifespan. There comes a time when every gay guy is overlooked and ignored in the world of gay bars and pickups. It will usually happen around forty. Forty-five is pushing it. Age will run away with all of your attractiveness, especially in the youth obsessed niche of a world that gaylife can be.

"It just works out that way, Len. Most of the men our age are already committed to relationships. Happily settled. Setting up housekeeping. And even you have to admit Christopher is gorgeous. Like JFK Junior, but blond."

"Well, yes, he is that."

"But, I have to admit sex with him the last couple of times has been like masturbating with your left hand. Interesting, but it feels odd. Like heading the wrong way on the expressway. I've realized that Christopher is of that breed who has taken full advantage of the traits he inherited from his father. Like Teddy Brewster he is a master manipulator. You know he's managed to work the cast and crew into a frenzy of efforts to please him. Meanwhile, he manages to take all the credit for everything they accomplish. I had no idea this job was going to be such a long term assignment when I took it. Or that so much re-writing was expected. And then I won't even receive credit? Would Doc Simon or Jerome Robbins allow that?"

"No, probably not. But Steven Sondheim, Bob Fosse, and George Abbott all were play doctors at various times in their careers."

"Ah, yes, but the word got out, didn't it? That's how you and I know about it. That good old Broadway grapevine. But that's not going to happen for me. My contributions to *Mrs. MacKenzie's Muddle* will be swept under a great big silent rug. Accomplishments will remain unsung. It isn't fair."

"Good God, and we actors are accused of being divas. JB, quit whining and just do the job. You agreed to the conditions, so live with it. Next time you'll negotiate a better deal, won't you?"

"The deal wasn't the point, Len. It was my questions about Teddy Brewster that got me into this. I needed to get close to the play to gather information. And that part has actually worked out." JB slipped into a French accent. "I believe, mon ami, that I have ascertained who it was that engineered the death of Monsieur Teddy Brew-es-ter."

"For Christ's sake, cut out the Hercule Poirot impression and tell me what you've found. Who's the killer, JB?"

"Believe it or not, Ronald Prescott."

"I don't believe it."

"Its true. He had everything required of the murderer."

JB held up his hand and dropped one finger. "He had motive. There was a good chance that he was going to be driven into bankruptcy by Teddy's return to the stage. If Teddy had continued as director the show was going to be a turkey big enough to float in the *Macy's* Parade. A two and a half hour dance recital? Egad. Ronald would have been destroyed, his production company busted, his reputation in shambles."

JB dropped another finger.

"Next, he had opportunity. Ronald was the one who found, and then handed over the lethal inhaler at that last rehearsal. And he is certainly capable of committing the crime. His cutthroat reputation precedes him."

"When it comes to cutting costs for theater scenery, yes, he's a cutthroat. He's a glorified accountant, JB. Hardly the type to kill. He'd just write off the loss and try to produce another show. Bankruptcy never stopped Flo Zigfield, or David Merrick. Broke is a chronic condition with show producers. Anyway, I heard he was wealthy in his own right. He could have financed the show without angels, so I've heard."

"But with the simple erasure of Teddy Brewster from the equation Ronald finds himself in the position of having a sure fire hit that will net him an even bigger fortune. That's enough motive to satisfy Lieutenant Kelly any day."

"Too bad you don't have anything more than all this conjecture. You need something that would place Ronald irrevocably in the middle of the crime. Where did he get the amyl-nitrite?"

"I suspect he stole it from Teddy himself. Teddy kept a supply at his apartment. In the bedside table, according to Jillian Morgan. Ronald was in the apartment right after Teddy's heart attack. He could have taken it then."

"How about if you could put him there. In the room. Actually doing the deed?"

"How would I do that?"

"If you could place him in the bedroom stealing the amyl then you have more than just suspicions. It becomes a rock solid circumstantial case. How about fingerprints? If he took the amyl his prints would be on the bedside table, wouldn't they? Or maybe even on the package of nitrite ampules themselves. That's what you need, JB. Something solid for Lieutenant Kelly to confront Ronald with."

"Absolutely, and a terrific idea. Len. But how do you suppose I'm going to get into Teddy's apartment to obtain said fingerprints?"

"Wouldn't Christopher help you?"

"I don't think so. He's quite satisfied with the police report that puts cause of death as simple heart failure."

"Then we need somebody else." Len put his brain to conjugating. "I know. Maybe Lee would help us."

"You think? But what would we tell her? We'll need an excuse?"

"How about you want to soak up the atmosphere of the place for that bogus book you're writing about Teddy?"

"Bogus? What makes you say that?"

"JB, you're a crime novelist, not a biographer. Unless there's a murder in Teddy Brewster's case you could care less. You wouldn't be interested in writing Brewster's life story."

"But saying I am has worked to get people talking."

"Maybe it will also work to convince Lee Arden to take you to Teddy's. Once you get in you could manage to be there alone somehow. Then you would have the time to take the fingerprints."

"Perfect. Humm. Len, you're closer to Lee than I am. Could you ask her for me? Just tell her what you said a moment ago. I know you could convince her. You can do that, can't you?"

"I suppose, but I wish I knew why I always help you in these escapades of yours."

"Because you're just as intrigued by them as I am. It's why we make such a good team. Holmes and Watson. Laurel and Hardy."

"More like *Glen or Glenda*."

Dance: Ten

Sixteen

While
Len went off to persuade Lee Arden to surrender the key
to Teddy's apartment, JB took the number six subway to
Grand Central, the shuttle across to Times Square, and
then caught the number one to the Christopher Street
Station in Greenwich Village. That left him only a few
blocks to walk to the alley off Jane Street that held The
Spy Shop.

JB had been there several months before when he had
needed a video camera. This time he was in search of a
fingerprinting kit. Expecting the same weasely clerk he
had found the last time he was surprised to be greeted by
an unknown gentleman. He was a garden gnome of a man
with a smile reminiscent of Alfred E. Newman of *MAD*

Magazine fame. Same protruding ears and gap in the front teeth.

The man greeted him politely and after inquiring of his needs directed JB to a cabinet at the back of the store. From it he pulled a dark wooden box about the shape and size of a cigarette carton. He laid that on the cabinet and explained, "This is our deluxe model." as he opened the box.

JB saw it contained a velvet lining holding several types of soft looking brushes in its lid. They were reminiscent of the make-up brushes he had seen in Len's dressing room. One was a big fluffy purple haired one; used the clerk explained for dusting. There were two jars each of what the clerk called lifting powders. There was one jar of white and one of dark. Another small jar held a clear liquid. Also there were several small manila envelopes. These contained clear plastic slips to pick up the powder once it had attached to the oil of the print itself. All pretty basic. And pretty expensive if the tag hanging off it was any sign. One hundred and eighty dollars seemed extreme.

"Could we look at something a bit less dear?"

The clerk sniffed. "Of course."

He shut the wooden box and returned it to the cabinet. Then he rummaged in the storage space below and pulled out a flimsy cardboard box the same size and shape as the wooden one. It held the same items as the one previously, except there was only one purple brush, a jar each of white and dark powders, a jar of clear, and a single envelope of the plastic slips. It only lacked the fancy presentation.

The salesman continued his pitch. "Once the prints are gathered you will need someplace to have them examined and compared. We can recommend an excellent technician."

JB leaned in to check out the kit. He opened up the printed instructions and glanced over them.

"I don't think it'll be necessary. I have a source already." He was thinking that whatever he was able to find Lieutenant Kelly could have his own lab check out. Why wouldn't he? Especially once it was explained what the prints stood to reveal?

JB paid the seventy-five dollars for the cheaper kit

and left the store. Then he wandered the Village for the rest of the evening looking into store windows that catered to the gay community.

Gay business was a newly discovered niche market that even large industries were now aiming for. Magazines like the *Advocate* and *Mandate* were packed with glossy advertisement's for cars, hotels, and especially the latest vodka to hit the market. Smaller business's had discovered gay spending power years before. Card shops, leather good's boutiques, restaurants, and book stores all benefited from the gay dollar. *Oscar Wilde Books*, a particular favorite, even had a display of JB's latest mystery stacked by their register. He signed four or five copies for the clerk—which guaranteed his royalty on them at the next quarter. Every sale helped and signed books couldn't be returned for a refund to his publisher.

Once back at home JB got out the kit and opened it. He gazed for a moment at the array of contents. Again he unfolded the printed instructions. They were short with instructions and heavy with warnings. JB then took each of the items from the box and laid them out before him. This can't be that hard, JB was thinking.

He pulled the plastic tea container he had taken from the kitchen counter closer and pressed his thumb and fingers on the hard black surface. Dipping the neon purple brush into the white powder, he dragged it across the place where he had pressed his thumb just moments before. The fine powder attached itself to the oils left behind by his finger and brightly highlighted the oval shaped print.

Excellent. JB then pulled out one of the clear plastic strips, separated the two layers and laid the sticky side down over the print. That all made sense, now didn't it?

But when JB tried to lift the strip, to preserve it, the damn thing wouldn't budge. As JB worked on it with his fingernails, the glue on the plastic strip would slither and skid over the surface of his favorite tea holder. It wouldn't come loose. Where was he going to put that pile of teabags in his kitchen if his tea caddy was ruined?

JB continued to worry at the slippery plastic strip and soon had the entire first half of it hanging off the edge of the caddy. Then, like some medieval trickery—or it could have been static electricity—the hanging sticky side of the strip jumped over to the other side of the container, bent, and stuck itself to that side. Damn. JB set it down on the table. Now what could he do? There was now a great big piece of tape cemented to two sides of his tea holder. Maybe he could face it toward the wall.

JB picked up the instructions and read them more carefully. There still wasn't much to be found on the technique of fingerprinting.

◈◈◈

The sticky tape incident occasioned JB's walk up Broadway on the Westside the next afternoon. That was after his latest quickie with Christopher. The man had called and JB had gone to his place right away. Like a lemming to his doom at the cliff's edge.

It was a part of himself that JB wasn't crazy about. This need he had to dance at somebody's attention. He would always drop his own projects to go running after the least little attention shown. Something from his childhood, he supposed. Something to share with his shrink.

JB, as he walked from Christopher's, decided that the attraction between them, by this point in their affair, had become completely physical. Still satisfying but becoming predictable and no where near as exciting as at the beginning.

JB walked up Broadway to the entertainment branch of the public library at Lincoln Center. Tucked behind Avery Fisher Hall, he walked past a narrow tiled still water pond that stretched along the way to the entrance. It was an island of calm in the city, in that it held several varieties of water flora with many reeds and lillypads. It, in its very stillness, seemed a signal that quiet was expected once inside the library building itself. The neo-Egyptian marble front loomed just ahead.

Bags were checked, then JB walked through an alarm arch and was in the lobby. Checkout was over to the right. Recordings, on disk with listening carrels that included turntables and headsets, were on the left. At the end of the burgundy carpeted hall, a right turn past several sets of wooden book shelves would bring him into the library proper.

This was where JB knew he could find instructions on the fine art of fingerprinting. And while he was there he could check the biography section for any information they might have on the illustrious Teddy Brewster.

The fingerprinting instructions he found by searching in the Crime and Punishment section. It explained the presence of the wax sealed glass bottle of alcohol in the kit he had brought home. It wasn't for cleaning up afterward, as JB had thought. It was meant to be used to dilute the glue on the sticky plastic strips. Which in turn, would allow them to be lifted. Good to know!

JB took the book to the copy machines, put in his quarters and copied the pages he wanted to review later. With that accomplished he started to wander the stacks, stopping occasionally to examine a title that looked interesting.

Buoyed by his inspection of the Dewey Decimal System card files JB walked the numbers as directed to the Musical Theater section. He found a shelf of books that mentioned Teddy, and copies on film of articles written about him. He also found a cabinet of file folders that held eight by ten pictures of Teddy. Both publicity shots and candids used by the press.

The information he found on Teddy Brewster leaned toward the career and tabloid speculation sort. Telling the tale of a selfish, eccentric, narcissist who had sold his very soul to show business. A man who had left a wake of tossed aside, no longer useful, benefactors and acquaintances laying prostrate behind him as he gained a career as a celebrated and honored maker of Art. It had also left him a not very generous or pleasant man to deal with. His career must have, in all ways, destroyed his very being. Was career the motor that drove Teddy Brewster? Was it that lust for fame that stole his humanity? Was there a lesson in there that people would be interested in?

JB had been thinking that maybe the bogus book he had been using to pry open people's memories would be a good idea to really write. Thank God people took pride in their run-ins with the famous. That desire to rub shoulders with the celebrated had netted him some very good information. In New York a meeting with someone famous could get you a years worth of dinner invites if you told it right. He was thinking that maybe a foray into autobiography, telling someone else's story, might be interesting. And possibly lucrative. After all, non-fiction always sold better than fiction, didn't it? Would Teddy's sordid life story capture the public's taste? Are you kidding? It could out sell the Bible— which has its own litany of scandals and sordid tales to recommend it. Well, he reconsidered, maybe not enough sales to beat religion. But, at the least, it would probably rake in the same numbers those Charles Higham bios on movie stars did.

JB looked through the files and found several folders with early photos inside. Old rehearsal shots of Teddy with his dancers. Taken at each show he had choreographed from that first specialty number in *The 1964 Passing Fancies Revue* Off-Broadway to his huge successes on the New York stages of the Nineteen-seventy's until the Nineteen-eighty's.

It was while JB was looking at photos from that earliest show that he found a startling image. It was a group shot of the entire cast and crew, with Teddy on one knee, Jolson style, arms akimbo, at the center. The chorus was lined up directly behind him, each holding their, even then, trademark tambourines at their breasts.

JB at first looked over the young faces until he found Lee Arden's. With dark hair—not the trademark white blond yet. *The 1964 Passing Fancies* would have been her first show with Teddy. It was the show that gave her the romantic dance with Teddy she mentioned at the wake. The next musical was the one with the dance number that stopped the show. That led her to the part in the next show. That one brought her lasting stardom.

But, JB then noticed, there was another person standing down the line from her in that long ago picture. He was twenty-five years younger, and the glasses weren't there to distort his features, nor the receding hairline, but it was Ronald Prescott. He was standing with the office crew, the secretaries and phone girls that kept every production humming along. That meant he was working the books even then. He looked eager instead of harried in Nineteen-sixty-four, but it was him all right.

So the man who JB suspected of murdering Teddy Brewster had an even longer history with his victim; a connection that went back to both their beginnings in show business. It was another brick on the wall of evidence that might eventually convict Ronald Prescott.

JB moved from the B drawers to the P's and found a similar file there on Prescott himself. JB carried that file to a gathering of tables, sat in one of the libraries straight back wooden chairs, and began to read from the articles and pictures he found inside.

Ronald Prescott had come to New York from a little town called Mawahawken, named after some obscure Indian tribe that had wandered the area a hundred years before. The town was located near the beach out on Long Island.

Ronald had arrived in New York mere months after Teddy had. The two men, who were said to have met on stage at a rehearsal of *The Passing Fancies*, developed an instant friendship. Ronald had been hired as an assistant to the stage manager but it was quickly discovered he had a talent for saving time and money on the production itself. It was at his suggestion that Teddy get his tambourines at *Toys-R-Us* instead of from a music store. The idea had saved them over a thousand dollars.

Soon after that, at Teddy's urging, Ronald moved into the offices and eventually into producing. Since he had taken several college courses in accounting it seemed a perfect fit. And it was. He came into his own once he began putting entire productions together. He was able to keep to a strict bottom line, and then look after the productions that Teddy dreamed up.

The two men had climbed the show business ladder together. Each one supplying what the other needed. With Lee Arden as Teddy's muse, and Ronald always there to curtail Teddy's more extravagant ideas, it became a winning combination. They had brought many successful and classic shows to the Broadway boards.

Even when Teddy seemed to go into decline, after Lee retired, Ronald Prescott stuck by him, loyal to a fault, even producing several shows that failed or had minimal runs. *Mrs. MacKenzie's Muddle* was an effort by Ronald to get his old friend back on top.

But that wasn't what was happening.

The most recent clippings in the file gave that story. *Mrs. MacKenzie's Muddle* had been troubled right from the beginning. It had taken all of Ronald's contacts to finance the show. And even then he had come up short. If it hadn't been for Lee Arden using her own funds the revival wouldn't have happened at all. Then, just weeks after rehearsals were begun, Teddy had his first heart attack. The production waited for him, and in two months he was back. But his second attack took him only a few months later. That had led to his bypass operation and finally his death. What was most disconcerting for everyone involved were the rumors of what Teddy was doing with the show. He was, it was reported, taking the show in very odd and unusual directions. He was choreographing erotic and lewd dance numbers to replace the bucolic charm of the original production. There were also angry fights between Teddy and the star, Betty Kane. Then Ronald, at the badgering of his co-producers, had to get involved in trying to soften Teddy's more drastic creations. That led to the two men not speaking with each other. Even Lee had stepped in to express her own doubts. Teddy had a fit. His constantly being pulled in all directions, along with his, by the end, almost maniacal insistence that his vision of the production be followed slavishly was believed to have led to that second heart attack. The show was being called the S&M version of *Little Nell,* with Nell taking rolls in the hay with all comers.

At Teddy's insistence the show was becoming the disaster that everyone expected it to be. And the critics would have loved taking another crack at Teddy. He had pissed off many of them when they had slashed his last two shows. Ads were taken and interviews were given by Teddy, who blasted them for their narrow vision and evil intentions. If Teddy had continued Ronald Prescott would have ended up with a damaged reputation and no chance of continuing his production company. Even if he had used his own money. That gave Prescott another motive. Another brick in that cell on Rikers Island.

Seventeen

◆◆◆◆◆◆◆◆◆◆◆◆◆◆◆◆ "Jeez, JB, I don't know why it was so easy. I asked Lee for the key to Teddy's apartment, like you said. Well, you knew she was gonna ask why. I told her that you wanted to soak up atmosphere for the book you were planning on Teddy, like you said. And she just handed the set of keys over to me?" Len held out the brass set of keys. "She even offered to call the doorman at the building to let him know you were coming. I let her. Is that okay?"

"I don't see why not? Anything to grease the wheels. Make it easier to get what I want."

"She acted like she was completely aware of this bogus book of yours. It is bogus, isn't it? I'm beginning to wonder. You haven't been BS'ing me like you've BS'd everyone

127

else?"

"Yes, it's bogus, Len. And I haven't talked to either Lee or Christopher about writing any such missive."

"Missive? Well, la-de-da, as Scarlett O'Hara once said."

"I'll bet one of the dancers went running to her about three seconds after I left the rehearsal hall the other day. Probably your Jimmy. I'd forgotten about the gossiping that a show cast indulged in. You did warn me. How did she take it? The book idea?"

"She didn't seem to hate it. But she did say she would have to speak with you too. Like the others."

"An interview about Teddy? I could do that. You know I did some research on him. He had a pretty tumultuous life. It could be enough for a book. Maybe a roman-a-clef to avoid libel. There are way to many people in his story that are still alive. But right now I need to focus on getting those fingerprints. You want to come with me?"

"Not really. Anyway, I have a date tonight. With Jimmy."

"You're still seeing him?"

"People who have clandestine rendezvous with straight directors shouldn't throw attitude, JB."

"What makes you say Christopher is straight?"

"There was an item in Cindy Adams column today. It said that Christopher is taking Belinda Fairfax-Warner to the opening preview of our show next week. They are, apparently, a hot item among the young eligibles about town. You remember her, JB? The striking young woman that opened the door at Lee Arden's. The day of the wake."

JB thought back and pictured a brittle young blond thing in a leotard and a flowered skirt who opened the door to them. Belinda Fairfax-Warner was the daughter of the very socially prominent Fairfax's and Warner's. Of the South Hampton, Connecticut, Park Avenue crowd. She was in Manhattan studying to be a dancer—girlhood fancies and all, as her indulgent family called them.

"Have you ever heard the word beard, Len? But, I'll admit he does seem confused. Obviously. And how many supposedly straight men have you bedded? You know as well as I do that there's a spectrum. Men range in degrees of homosexual desire along a scale. There's exclusively straight all the way to flamboyantly gay. From all appearances Christopher is dancing somewhere in the middle. He just hasn't been completely honest with himself. Yet. Was coming out all that easy for you?"

"To quote our own Mrs. MacKenzie script...'I haven't done anything as nature intended'. I just was. There was never a question. I arose from the sea as Venus did"

"On the half-shell, I suppose? Like in the painting?"

"JB, Christopher needs to have a serious talk with himself. And quickly. Before he does something stupid, like marrying that girl. He could end up destroying both their lives. You need to talk to him, JB."

"So you think I should tell Christopher Brewster— the son of one of the most sexually liberated and amoral straight men on the Broadway scene of the Sixties and Seventies—that he's gay? Christ, Teddy Brewster made Warren Beatty look like a choir boy. And I'm supposed to tell his son that he should admit to being a huge homo to the entire press corps that will be attending the opening of his fist Broadway show? Not such a sterling idea when its all spelled out, is it, Len?"

"You know, JB, sometimes apples can fall quite far from their trees. Christopher needs to make a decision. And you need to shake a limb or two of his to do it. It's your responsibility to, at the least, make him look at what he's doing. At the possible consequences. And there are consequences."

"I know you're right, Len, but its the kind of talk I really shy away from. It's such a personal thing. Every guy has to do it for himself. I'll bet even Richard Simmons had a few questions about himself."

"And how much easier would it have been if he had a guide. Someone to support him on the journey. You've got to do it, JB."

"I'll think about it, okay?"

JB got into his coat and scarf. He put his cap on, checked the hall mirror, and said, "I'll see you at rehearsal then? Watch out on your date tonight. I don't want you getting taken. 'My dope was duped. Or is it they duped my dope...'"

"Barbra Streisand, *Funny Girl*, Columbia, 1968. You

can't fool me."

"Never could." He went over and hugged Len. Then he left to go to Teddy's apartment.

Teddy had lived on the East Side. More comfortable to carry on as he wished with Central Park between him and his ex-wife. His place was in the Fifties, just off Madison. With a canopied entrance and a twenty-four hour doorman. The doorman was a rotund man with a field of brass buttons parading down his coat front. He reached up and shifted his hat on his head.

"Yeah, I got a call about you. Take the elevator to the third floor. Down the hall to your left. Number three-o-six. Let me know when ya leave, okay?"

JB answered, "Sure." and went to the elevator.

Teddy's door was painted red, but the metal fronting it had been scratched with keys or other sharp instruments. A set of three locks were one on top of another at the right.

With Teddy's keys in his hand JB was inside like butter. Was that from *Funny Girl* too? He'd have to ask Len.

There were signs in the one bedroom apartment that someone, Lee probably, or the police, had made an inspection of the place. Items were askew. There were untidy stacks of papers on the desks. Then again, maybe Teddy was just a slob?

JB made his way into the bedroom. It didn't look as disturbed as the outer room. But the bed took up a big part of the space. You scooted to get around in there. JB went to the bedside table that Jill had said held Teddy's amyl nitrite supply. He opened it.

Inside was the usual collection of bedside items. Half empty matchbooks, remotes for TV and music, an ashtray, and a matchbox sized cardboard box of a dozen gauze covered amyl nitrite ampules. Inside there were still ten ampules left. The date on the box had the prescription last filled a few days before Teddy's last heart attack. Given that he might have used one ampule before his attack that still left one missing. The one that Ronald took?

JB got out his fingerprinting kit and set it up on the bed. He dipped into the jar of amino black powder with the purple brush and began testing it. He tested not only the box he was holding, but also the polished veneer drawer front and the top edge of the bedside table itself. He worked quickly, the powder smearing and settling to show previous users print remnants unwillingly, but inevitably, left behind.

He found a single print on the little box, and three different sets of prints on the front of the drawer. One of them, one could guess, was Teddy's. Another, that looked smaller, daintier, might be Jillian's. And there was a very nice clear thumb print JB found that could belong to the culprit he was looking for. But why only the thumb? Thumbs are attached to four other appendages. Where were they?

JB opened the jar of dark powder again and started dusting the untreated wood inside the front of the drawer. Sure enough, there were four fingerprints on that side of the drawer. He diluted the glue on the plastic pickup slips with a Q-Tip and removed each of the four prints, plus the three on the front of the drawer and the one on the box. He stored them in his backpack for examination as soon as he could get them to Kelly's precinct.

Meanwhile, Len was meeting Jimmy at a coffee shop near Lincoln Center. They were going to a movie later. "What movie are we talking about?" Len asked.

Jimmy smiled his most sparkling. "I stopped at Equity today. They had tickets for a special screening. I managed to get two."

"Gad, I haven't done that in years. I saw some terrific stage shows with Equity tickets." Producers often would paper a theater or a screening by handing out passes at the Actors Equity offices. Problem was they tended to go to the upper echelon officers before the rank and file had a chance at them. If they were still left after they had their pickings the show Jimmy was proposing could be a real drag. "That could be great. What movie are we talking about?"

"Something called *The Last Emperor*. Have you heard of it?"

"Bertolucci's new film? You snagged a goodie, luv. I adore foreign directors. Especially with the budget Bernardo had. The entire Chinese government was behind him. I read in *Variety*, that they kept Queen Elizibeth out of the Forbidden City so he could film."

"Its due for release next year, but they want to gauge audience reaction. We'll get it at its first edit, so it may be a long evening. And we'll have to fill out a questionnaire after. Is that okay?"

"It's my night off and I enjoy your company. Of course it's okay."

They both felt the presence of another warm body hovering over them. They turned and looked up at the waitress waiting to take their order. They went ahead and ordered just sodas and dessert, anticipating popcorn at the movie.

Jimmy took a sip of his cola and said to Len. "I was looking at some nice things this afternoon. At one of the antique stores you took me to. Prices were at the top of my range, but there were a few smalls I got for the collection."

The collection that Jimmy was mentioning had become the proverbial elephant with his foot in the middle of their friendship. The mention of it would lead directly to Jimmy asking what Len had decided about the loan he had asked for. As they were finishing their desserts Jimmy finally had enough chitchat and asked outright if Len was going to lend him the cash.

Len decided to equivocate a bit longer. "I'm not saying I'm not interested, but I do wonder..." Len hesitated. He didn't like calling anyone on their business abilities. But JB had raised some well-deserved red flags. "Uh, what I wonder about is your being able to make a profit. And JB had questions too..."

"What did he want to know? And what business is it of his?"

"He's my best friend, Jimmy. He worries about me. He wanted to know why you hadn't saved money for opening this business you talk about? Apparently for years. I know. Its none of his business. But I think I want to know too."

"I'm pretty sure I can answer both of your questions. Are you finished with your dessert?"

Jimmy started to slip out from the booth they were sitting in.

As Len lifted a last bite of pie, he said, "Just a moment, where are we off to? And what time do we have to be at the movie theater?"

Jimmy was caught mid-slide. "I have a storage locker near here I want you to see. And we have plenty of time before the picture."

Len left the tip and slid after Jimmy.

"How close are we talking?"

Jimmy was wrapping his scarf. A flip and a throw and it fell artistically about his neck. Len reminded himself to ask him how he did that. It looked like a move from something Fred Astaire or Clifton Webb would have pulled off in one of their movies. So smooth. But that was one of the more attractive things about Jimmy. He was so polished. So facile. So slick. He was so well turned out it was almost intimidating.

"Its just behind the old Coliseum. And the movie is showing at the *Lowes* in Columbus Circle, so it's all right in the neighborhood."

"Admit it. You're a Westsider in disguise. You know this neck of the woods far too well."

"All right, I admit it. When I first got to New York I stayed here, in this neighborhood, with a friend for the first eight months. Then I got a place of my own, still here, over at Eighty-fifth and Broadway. That's when I first started going to the antique stores. There used to be a whole bunch of them on Amsterdam and Columbus just a few years ago. That's when I rented the locker. My place wasn't big enough to hold what I was picking up."

They were by then standing in front of a pre-war building built from a dusty rose colored brick. Accenting the window casings were deeper, redder bricks. Below it was a modern locked grill covering the windows. Jimmy swiped a plastic card and pushed on the door. They waited at the inside window while the guard checked their ID's and then, after being buzzed in, went down a wide wooden hall with heavy oak doors lining each side.

Jimmy's voice echoed in the vast two story hallway. "I would drag my treasures here so I didn't have to carry them such a long way. Especially after I moved over to the East Side. I was that crazy guy lugging a Louie Napoleon chaise down the street."

Jimmy opened the last door on the hall and stood

aside.

"Well, really this is more like two eight foot high plaster and lathe rooms," he said following Len inside.

Len was flabbergasted. The two rooms were piled high with some of the most exquisite pieces of antique furniture Len had ever seen. Even lined along the rooms of the Metropolitan Museum's American collection. All of it was placed against the walls as if it was on display in that shop Jimmy always meant to open.

Len had taken an antique appraising class at *The New School*. Because of that he could see that many of the pieces were American Federal along with a mixture of Victorian and Edwardian period pieces. Heavy velvet drapes backed them giving their settings a stagey feel. And there were several twenties Deco pieces mixed in, complete with all the accessories, layered mirrors, magazine holders, a stand alone ashtray. Even crocheted doilies on the overstuffed arms of a Morris chair.

That's interesting, Len was thinking. If he's bought Deco furniture then why didn't he see that the piece in my apartment was a fake? He would have to ask.

More mirrors in ornate frames lined the upper walls along with some good Seventeenth and Eighteenth century paintings. There was a grouping of crystal chandeliers hanging at the center. Len, looking up into them, felt he had been transported to some distant fairyland.

"It's wonderful, Jimmy. Where in God's name did you find all this?"

"Like I said, here in the neighborhood. This is where all of my money has gone, Len. If this shop is going to work, I have to fill it, and keep it filled with more things just like this. I have to be my own picker. Lately I've found some really good things out in Brooklyn."

Len sat at an ormolu desk and ran his hands over the brass studded leather of the top.

"Where are you planning on opening your shop."

"I would love to be on Madison Avenue, but it's way too expensive. I was thinking, maybe down in the Village. Over toward Second. Or on Houston."

"Why not Madison Ave?" Len looked around. "These goods are for the carriage trade, my dear. You'll have to talk to a real estate broker. I know someone. I'll make an appointment for us to see him."

"Does that mean you going to loan me the money?"

"It means I'm willing to explore our options. Let's not put horses and carts together just yet."

◈ ◈ ◈

JB handed over the envelope containing the fingerprints from Teddy's apartment. Kelly opened the flap and peeked inside.

"What is it you want from me, Bent?"

"I was wondering if you could have those analyzed and identified?"

"I'm supposed to use my lab to read what are probably unauthorized prints, taken by an amateur, for a case that doesn't even exist."

"As a favor."

"Come on, give. What is this going to prove?"

"I believe if these prints can be identified as belonging to the person I think it is, you will have the killer of the late, great, Teddy Brewster."

Kelly sat up straight. "You have proof that he was murdered?"

"What I have is a strong circumstantial case for you and the district attorney to prove. These prints are from the bedside table in Teddy's bedroom. It should implicate the person I suspect by proving that he stole an ampule of amyl nitrate, which was used to cause Teddy Brewster to have his fatal heart attack. Is that good enough for you?"

"Who is it you suspect?"

"If I tell you then you won't check the prints. Please, Kelly, what you have there will give you a stronger case."

"It'll take a day or two. Even making it a priority will take that long."

"I can wait. Can you? I'm sure you wonder who it might have been?"

"I looked into this group. Teddy Brewster was not a very well liked man by a lot of people. It could have been any one of them. His ex-wife, his kid, his mistress, his actors, his producer. Hell, his cleaning-lady hated him for the sloppy house he kept."

"Well, the person I have in mind had all the basics.

There was opportunity, motive, witnesses, and those prints will put him actually taking the murder weapon. Other than a confession what more do you want?"

"So, I can rule out the ex-wife and the mistress since you said 'him'?" He rubbed his jaw. "I have a newbie down in the lab. He's always eager to please. I'll put him on it. I'll call you when I get the results."

"Thanks, Kelly. You're a peach."

"What I am is a prickly pear. And I'm busier than hell, Bent. Get out of my office so I can work. Oh, and Bent, thanks for not making a mess of this. Good work."

It was the closest Kelly had ever been to passing out a compliment.

"Well, thank you, Lieutenant. I'll remember this moment."

"What the hell? You queer? Oh yeah, you are. Sorry, it was an automatic reaction."

"And there is the problem. You think its okay that derogatory gay terms are all right to use whenever you feel like it. Each of them is like a stab to the chest. They hurt, Kelly."

"Geez, save it for the gay parade. Now get the hell out of here."

He bent over his files.

◼ig**ighteen**

◆◆◆◆◆◆◆◆◆◆◆◆◆◆◆◆◆◆I t
was later that week that Kelly called JB and asked him to
come in to see him. Well, what he actually said was, "I want
your butt here in my office. Now!"

Such succinct wording of Kelly's message on JB's
answering machine had convinced JB that he should hang
up the phone in the theater lobby where he was checking
his messages, leave the rehearsal he was then attending,
and make his way to the police station post haste.

◆◆◆

JB was at the station in only a few minutes. Kelly
made him wait. The chairs outside Kelly's cubical were
standard city issue. JB had seen them before. Molded

plastic supported by thin chrome legs similar to that of a spider. Utilitarian. Uncomfortable.

JB waited an agonizing ten minutes. His ass had gone numb at three. It wasn't in his nature to sit and waste time, so he pulled out a notebook and wrote notes to himself for inclusion in his next project. What that might be was anybody's guess. Maybe a play? If that hinted at meeting with Ronald Prescott should come to fruition? Although, it wasn't looking so good for Ronald right that moment. If JB's suspicions were correct Mr. Ronald Prescott, Broadway impresario, could be spending his next production in Sing-Sing, waiting for the results of his last appeal.

Kelly finally came out of his office with another man. They moved away a few feet and Kelly, his arm around the fellow in bon homme fashion, leaned in and spoke into his ear. Then he turned abruptly and beckoned JB to enter his office. He stepped aside to let him go first. JB didn't feel like doing the *No, you first*...dance, so he went through the door. Once inside he sat in the chair in front of Kelly's desk. Kelly stepped behind his desk, sat, straightened his tie, and said, "Now, these prints..." He held up an envelope. "... where did you say they came from?"

"From just where I told you before. The bedside table where Teddy Brewster kept his amyl nitrite capsules. What did you find? Who's are they?"

"We found an unknown on the box, which meant we had to identify it with a background check. There was also a print from Brewster's mistress..." He checked the file in front of him, "Jillian Monroe. And, there were prints from Ronald Prescott. Prescott's thumb was on the front of the drawer and the four fingerprints from the inside were his too. Also, yours were among the prints, but I figured you were using a control print for the lab."

"Actually it had more to do with a tea caddy I have at home. It wasn't supposed to be there. Sorry."

"I did run an arrest report on the unknown print for you." He leaned back in his chair. Talking to the ceiling he said, "That came up with something very interesting." Now he was looking straight at JB. "Does the name Theodore Brewinski mean anything to you?" JB shook his head. "The print from the box came up with that name. It was a match from a local police report out in Nassau County. The original was taken as a school kids fingerprinting initiative back in the Fifties"

"Well, that print was on the box, right? It had to be Teddy's. I'll bet he changed his name early in his career. A lot of people in show business do. And they always tend to use their same initials. Easier to remember, I guess."

"I can see why this kid changed his."

Kelly handed over a fax of several pages from a police blotter dated April, Nineteen-fifty-two from the township of Mawahawken. Where had JB seen that name before?

It held the record of this Theodore Brewinski kid. He had evidently been a very bad boy. From the age of ten to the age of nineteen he had been arrested and charged so many times that the only thing left for him as an adult was to get arrested for a capital crime. Through the years he had committed both petty and major thefts in and around the lakeside summer houses of the New York millionaires that vacationed at the beach houses out there on Long Island. He had even spent a short stint in prison, after he had outgrown the juvenile homes. Theodore was always the kid that got caught.

It got worse. In Nineteen-fifty-two—when he was twenty—was the year of Theodore's arrest for the murder of a local woman, a servant to one of the rich residents. She was killed during a robbery of their home by three boys.

Theodore had been the boy on the outside, the driver of the getaway car. When he was caught he had steadfastly refused to give up the names of the other two boys. They, he said, were the ones who had instigated the robbery.

He told his story to the jury at his trial for the cleaning woman's murder. Under cross examination he explained that he thought the other two boys were only going to carry out a fraternity tradition. Some prank involving a stuffed goat's head. And since he was flattered that classmen at the local college, guys older than him, were interested in being his friend, he went along with their plan. These two upper classmen were supposed to only be getting the mascot from the president's office. Theodore didn't know there was anyone inside the house. The place was supposed to be empty. The cleaning woman had discovered the two boys while they were robbing the president's safe and had been killed for that discovery. He said he didn't even know the boy's had a gun. "It had nothing to do with me" he begged.

The jury believed him and acquitted.

Once he was free of the charges he left town, never to be seen in those parts again, as the saying goes. His landlady kept his belongings for the required ninety days and then sold them to the trashman. Theodore Brewinski was essentially wiped off the face of the earth. And, by JB's reckoning, a few months later was reborn as Teddy Brewster, dancer. "

JB looked over at Kelly.

"Like I said, Brewster must have changed his name. But the date on this report is wrong. Teddy was supposed to be out in Hollywood trying to be the next Gene Kelly in Nineteen-fifty-two. This all happened in a town out on Long Island." JB waited for the thought to click. "You know what? I'll bet Teddy left that town and came here to New York City to lose himself. Can you blame him? Conservative Fifties. Uptight Long Island. I would have run too. Maybe not for the same reasons, but certainly the same motive. That's why New York City is so perfect. You can disappear here. Even recreate yourself." JB pulled himself back from a flash of memory—his own escape from Kansas all those years ago—and looked back over at Kelly. "So, Teddy arrived here, told a small lie about his past, and I won't even try to explain how, but got cast in that first show. Then he proceeded to invent a new him. A new person. He was no longer the kid who was charged with murder, not the messed up rebel with a reason if not a cause. Instead he became Teddy Brewster, dancer."

Kelly rubbed at his chin, considering. "I have to admit it makes sense. Actors change their faces for a living. Besides, all the other prints you gave us check out clean. You should also know we are in the process of contacting Mr. Prescott right now as to the reason his prints were on Brewsters nightstand. And to question him about the suspicious circumstances of Teddy Brewster's death."

"Kelly, would it be possible to check on the background of one more person. A man named Jimmy Jameson."

Kelly bent over and made a note.

"Is he involved in the murder?"

"Oh, no, I meant as another favor. He's involved with a friend of ours. Len. To be honest, I think he's a bit greasy. Even Broadway can have its share of sleaze-balls and con-men. Just ask Damon Runyon."

Kelly agreed with a nod. "Len is involved?"

This time JB nodded.

"All right, I'll put the name in. But this time you'll pay for it. I want a donation to the Police Children's Fund."

"You got it."

Kelly bent over his desk and opened a folder. After a moment he looked up. "You still here?"

JB said, "I was hoping to listen in on the questioning of Prescott."

"Are you kidding? This is police business. You are not invited. This is a police case and a police arrest."

"Using evidence I..."

"Supplied? Okay, I'll give you that. But it only served to send our valiant police force on the search that will solve the case. Your little contribution is much appreciated."

"Kelly, you wouldn't even have a murder if it wasn't for me. I've given you a chance at a promotion, you ungrateful son of..."

"Yes."

"I don't use that kind of language in even your rough company. But, when they hand you that new badge, and put Captain in front of your name, don't forget where that raise in pay grade came from. I'll use it when other favors might be needed."

JB stood and left the office. He meant to head for home, but instead got into a taxi and directed it to an address on the Upper East Side.

Settling in the cab he was thinking. What's interesting about this new information is the town of Mawahawken. Ronald Prescott, in those articles he'd read at the library, was from the same town as this Theodore Brewinski. Or rather Teddy Brewster. And they were both the same age, so Prescott was probably there in Mawahawken when the kids murder trial was going on. That's a connection, isn't it? If Brewinski and Brewster were the same person it might be the reason Prescott had risen so fast as a producer. Teddy had aided in that, hadn't he? Prescott's rise as a producer had been seen as almost meteoric. He had even been called a *wunderkind* in those early days, a term usually reserved for the likes of an Irving Thalberg or Orson Welles in the movies. What if Prescott's fast rise was because of a little blackmail on his part? Did it cause Teddy to use his influence to get Prescott ahead. Wouldn't Teddy have paid to keep his true past hidden?

Maybe he should go to Mawahawken and check all this out. He'd have time for such a trip after the show tonight. After his job with *Mrs. MacKenzie's Muddle* was finally done. A trip to a quiet seaside enclave in winter might be just the retreat he needed. It would give him some time to figure out his next move. To decide what to do about Christopher for one thing. How to confront him over his seeing both Ms. Fairfax-Warner and him. He could walk the beach. He could get his mind around what he needed to do next.

The cab pulled over to the curb on Lexington at Seventy-sixth. "This close enough?"

JB looked around. "Sure." He got out and went to the front door of the corner apartment building. The uniformed doorman for the building was under the awning, standing with his arms spread, trying to hold back a small crowd that had formed around him.

Looking over the top of the crowd JB could see a prone body lying in the lobby of the building. A man was down. JB could see the fallen man was being attended to by another man who kneeled beside him. They were the only people on the inside. JB, when the kneeling man looked up, recognized him. It was the guy Kelly had spoken to outside his office before talking with JB earlier. He had undoubtedly been the one sent to pick up Prescott for questioning.

JB slipped past the doorman who was busy with his own problems. He was telling a loudly protesting woman that she should cross the street if she wanted to go past the building. The woman disagreed. Loudly and in the sort of voice that makes one wonder why any straight men would want to shackle themselves to such a harpy.

JB opened the door of the lobby and went over to the policeman. "Is he okay?"

Murder: Maybe?

The cop looked up. His eyes were glassy, and he was very pale. In a monotone he explained that he had asked Mr. Prescott to come down to the station. "That was all. He got real nervous and started sweating."

"Trust me, it wasn't you. The man will spritz over a torn fingernail."

By this time, JB had realized that the man lying on the ground, the man whose forehead the policeman was dabbing with a handkerchief was Ronald Prescott.

"He's is a spritzer."

Prescott moaned.

"Then, when we were in the elevator he started complaining about his arm hurting. He went down when we hit the lobby."

"Then he's alive, and he's probably having a heart attack."

"The doorman called nine-one-one."

"Good God, man, Lenox Hill Hospital is right across the street." JB bent down. "Help me lift him."

The two men held Prescott in their arms and stood up.

"Sir," the policeman said. "there are procedures."

"Screw them. This man's life is in jeopardy. We're taking him across the street. The emergency room is about a half block down. Now, come on. Move it."

JB and the policeman carried Prescott past the crowd at the entrance, across busy Lexington Avenue—where, by some miracle, they made the lights—and then the half block to the care of the Lenox Hill ER staff.

It was twenty minutes later that the doctors declared Ronald Prescott, Broadway producer—and all would agree a real mensch of a guy—was dead.

The policeman, who had waited at the hospital, called his boss and reported the death. He listened for a moment then turned to JB, standing next him.

"The Lieutenant wants to know if there's a murder in this one too?"

◆◆◆

JB stood in front of Lieutenant Kelly's desk while the older man glowered up at him. It wasn't a pleasant conversation. Kelly's jaw snapped as he tried, not very well, to hide his mounting anger. JB was still a citizen and people who lived in glass offices shouldn't abuse others, so he had to hold it in. He was mostly unsuccessful.

"So," he grunted, "your imaginary murder case is closed. As if it never even existed."

"Oh, don't you believe it, Kelly. This wasn't some figment of my imagination."

"Maybe you need to take a few days off from your novels, Bent. That imagination thing can get you in lots of trouble."

"You know, I was just thinking that same thing. To get out of town for a few days."

"Take a month. Please. It would be a pleasure not to have you around for awhile. Oh, here's that background on the Jameson guy you asked for." He held out the pages.

JB reached for them. Kelly held on to them.

"Wait a minute, where's that check for the kids?"

"Of course." JB reached into his backpack and grabbed his checkbook. He bent to write out the donation. While he did, he said, "I'm telling you, Lieutenant, Teddy Brewster was murdered. We had the proof."

"The DA it turns out had some real doubts about the strength of the case, Like everybody in her office, she was only interested in an airtight case that she could win. Your case was all suspicions, Bent. The evidence, if you want to call it that, was tenuous at best, based on the idea that Prescott had stolen the amyl nitrite. What got you there anyway?"

"He was the one who found Teddy's inhaler and returned it to him at that last rehearsal. Teddy had made a big scene about it. But when he got it he didn't use it. That was odd. After making such a big ta-doo about having it. I got that information from the chorus kids that were there and saw it. Otherwise, Teddy would have died at that moment, right there in the rehearsal hall. Instead, he died an hour later on Columbus Avenue."

"Again, it's flimsy. Prescott might have been the one who found the inhaler after it had been placed exactly where he would find it. Another person all together could have tampered with the inhaler and then put it somewhere easily found."

"You mean Prescott just happened to be the one who did find it? Much to his regret, I would think."

JB handed over the check. Kelly let go of the papers.

"You know what that means?" JB said. "There could be another murderer out there, Kelly. The person who really killed Teddy Brewster is still at large."

"Bent, damn it, there is no case. There are only your suspicions. Straight out of that devious twisty little mind of yours. Making up murders all the time. So, you found your pretend culprit and he's paid the price for his pretend sin. Now go home and write about it in your next book. Get the hell out of here."

"I do have to go. *Mrs. MacKenzie's Muddle* has its first preview tonight. I can't miss it. Its a Broadway opening. There'll be celebrities, and paparazzi, and even a critic might slip in. It should be very festive."

"Lots of overtime for the patrol boys to watch the watchers of the people arriving. Look out for the horseshit."

Meaning the mounted police would be running security in front of the theater that night.

When JB got to the street the first thing he did was stop and read over the background check Kelly had run on Jimmy Jameson.

When he finished reading he turned and went back into the police station.

Dance: Ten

ineteen

An opening of any show, even one in previews, is eagerly awaited by Broadway affectionatos. *Mrs. MacKenzie's Muddle* was that night having its first run in front of a paying audience. The first of two weeks of preview performances before the official opening night. That was scheduled for the first week in January. The timing couldn't be better, what with Christmas vacations and visitors to New York for the season the theater would be packed, creating much word-of-mouth for the show.

A few years before the musical would have been having its premier in New Haven or Cleveland on its way to New York. To get the kinks out of the show out of sight of the

New York critics. But recession style economics and fewer people attending the theater had reared its Gorgonesque head. Out of town was far too expensive on already tight and inflated budgets. The answer was that a production would now have its previews in New York before opening night, with it understood that the critics were not to review before then. Yeah, right. If they didn't slyly say something in their own columns, then the gossip press took up the torch. Look at the debacle that was Merrick's musical of *Breakfast At Tiffany's*. That show closed after only a few preview performances. Word of mouth was so bad it shut down before it even opened.

True, *Mrs. MacKenzie's Muddle* was a revival—meaning the material was tested and tried—which would go a long way to gaining acceptance for this new production. However, one had to consider there was a new cast, a new song, and a new sub-plot to be reckoned with. It was essentially a new show with familiar tunes. Luckily the casting of not one but two great ladies of the Broadway theater had generated a great deal of talk around town. Not to mention that the nasty death of the director had given folks something to wag about too. That meant there was buzz about the show in the papers and on the streets for the last several weeks. All to the good. For as the saying goes, any talk is better than none at all.

That first night the front of the house was packed with wishers—both well and ill—ebbing and waving, flowing and drifting their way to their seats before the curtain would go up. First night audiences at this sort of event were usually made up of friends, fans, and the backers with their wives. They also were not a very good judge of the material. Every joke got a huge laugh. Rapturous applause greeted each favored performer. If you were the director—or the writer—you were listening for glitches. Flat jokes, inattention from the audience, places to punch it up or tone it down. That sort of input wasn't what they would receive that night. What they did get, once the curtain went up, was a complete love fest, a fandamonium. The audience was acting like it was a *Judy at the Palace* concert.

Also, to add another element to the show that night, the cast was well aware the director was attending. That would at least guarantee a fairly straight forward performance from the actors. Rehearsed bits and line readings were stuck to this first time through. The first time playing is in essence the directors show, perhaps his only opportunity to present his own particular vision. Before the producers, the writers, the opinions of respected colleagues, and the press all begin having a say into what is being played.

There were the usual bitchy questions. Would it be a hit? Would it prove Christopher Brewster, the untried son of the late choreographer, a creative director? A lot was riding on this first performance.

JB stood it as long as he could, and finally had gone backstage to escape the tensions out front.

Backstage, however, was a shambles in its own right.

The news that Ronald Prescott, their producer, had died had shocked the entire cast and crew. Christopher, advised of the tragedy, had already stepped in and gathered the cast together. He reminded them that it was Ronald who had brought the show this far, making all the hard work they had done worthwhile. The show should go on, to paraphrase the Irving Berlin dictum.

It was decided to dedicate that evening's performance to Ronald's memory. A show of hands and Len was chosen to go in front of the curtain, in costume, before the overture, to announce the decision to the audience. There was a gasp from the crowd, and then mumbling as Len, looking spectral and shadowed by the footlights, explained the sudden and sad circumstances for the dedication. He finished and made his way off stage.

That done the orchestra began to prepare for the overture; the baton was raised, instruments were up. Then the conductor, instead of giving the downbeat, bent to listen to his headset. He halted the first notes and the musicians put down their instruments. The curtain was being called for the moment.

◆ ◆ ◆

The police had Jimmy Jameson by the arms and were guiding him along the hallway to the stage door. One of the officers was reciting his Miranda rights to him.

Most of the cast, including Len, were unaware it was even happening. They were already in place, on stage, waiting for the curtain to rise.

Again Christopher had to leave his fifth row seat and go backstage to the rescue. He was told what had happened and quickly recruited the assistant dance director to take Jimmy's place in the chorus for the evening. Nothing was going to stop the show.

"Another openin', another show...."

JB waited in Len's dressing room.

He knew that when Len found out what had happened to Jimmy he needed to be there to explain. He really wasn't sure how Len was going to take the information. The revelations the background check had unearthed about Jimmy were very serious. And JB wasn't sure just how deeply involved Len was in his affair with him. Or what kind of affair it was. Len had been quite nonchalant when they had talked before, but so had JB been when he was discussing Christopher.

To be truthful JB's affair with Christopher was cooling way down. Passion was proving itself once again fleeting, wearing thin quickly once spent. JB had not been able to completely accept Christopher's ambiguity concerning his sexuality. Was he in the closet or out? And when he had seen Christopher with that Ballinchine dance stick on his arm out in the lobby that evening it had made up his mind for him. He wasn't going to continue dancing to Christopher's beckoning calls. He wasn't cut out for old-time scenarios out of Fannie Hurst novels. He would still have to have that talk Len had encouraged him to have and that could seriously effect their relationship. It was possible that Christopher was perfectly content telling himself a great big lie. That he wasn't gay and was only "experimenting" with JB. If that was the case then JB had to end their affair. JB only hoped they would remain friends, but the hot as molten lava phase was over. Now all he had to do was tell Christopher.

Len was in a flurry when he came into his dressing room. There was a costume change to be made. JB stayed over in a corner, out of the dresser's way. The man was a member of the stagehand's union. And a vicious queen if ever there was one. JB let him do his job. Len, with the dresser fussing and fluffing behind him, was gone in moments.

JB sat back down. All he had heard while Len played the dervish, was that the audience was "loving it, laughs galore. Where the hell is that damn neckerchief?"

Obviously, the news about Jimmy hadn't been passed on yet. That was a relief. It gave JB more time to figure out what to tell Len.

As to the audience's reaction? It held little interest. After all, JB's work on the show was finished. The additional scenes he had been contracted to write were composed, approved by the director, and were being performed as written and rehearsed while he sat there and waited. He had fulfilled his contract and was no longer under the hire of the production company.

Rewrites would probably start when that evening's performance was over. In fact, he knew a meeting had been called for midnight. Pastrami sandwiches had been ordered. JB had been apprised of it, but had not decided if he would attend. There were monetary issues to be discussed first. Christopher had been taking advantage of JB's lust and been paying him far below what was standard for a Broadway show doctor. Admittedly, JB was no Neil Simon—who had come in and saved so many Broadway shows he was nicknamed Doc—but JB deserved more than what he'd signed on for.

He had decided not to watch that night's performance. Instead he could get any direction he needed from the audience after the show. You could glean most of the attitudes from that milling after show crowd. He would watch the body language used while delivering their opinions to their friends. That would indicate if the producers had a bomb or a viable show. You'd get a sense if or when the show lagged, or if it rose too high. A play, and a musical especially, is supposed to be a composed and harmonious whole. This isn't Stravinsky country. It needed to be more like Gershwin. To flow along gently, with provision made for the eleven o'clock closer.

JB knew if he went to that meeting he was looking at a long night of tweaks to the script. Move a song here, you

need a new introduction for it. A joke didn't work, you need
to write another. But, before any of that would happen JB
had a trick up his sleeve. Some might think it dirty, taking
advantage of the last minute circumstances as he was. JB
figured it was a simply a negotiation tactic, the same as
had been pulled on him countless times.

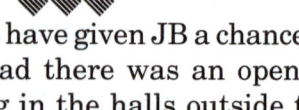

Intermission should have given JB a chance to talk with
Len about Jimmy, instead there was an open door policy
that let everyone milling in the halls outside the dressing
room come in and talk with Len. While he and his make-up
person re-applied his base for the second act Christopher
came in with some notes. Len's dresser interrupted and
asked about a quick change that had to be done just off
stage in the next act. And the musical director came back
with notes for each of the performers. JB had little choice
but to sit quietly sipping a soda from a can. The talk with
Len about Jimmy's arrest would have to wait.

Before Christopher left the room he stopped to talk
with JB, and affirmed what JB had expected the rest of the
evening would be like. There was work to be done on the
script Christopher said.

"Christopher, you realize my contract only went so far as
the initial re-write. There is no provision for my continuing
to work on this project after this first performance."

"What do you mean? You're not saying you want a new
contract? Now?"

"As a matter of fact, yes. I was speaking to a few other
writers and the going rate for what I've been doing is a lot
more than you've been paying me."

Christopher leaned in and whispered. "But we had an
arrangement."

"Business and pleasure are soon parted, to quote the
Bard. Before I do any more re-writing I think you might
want to make me a better offer."

"Better than what we've been doing to each other?" His
eyebrows waggled in a Groucho like fashion.

JB smiled. "I'm afraid you overestimate your own
value."

Christopher blustered a little bit, but saw that JB was
not going to give in. He sighed, pulled out a notepad and a

pencil from his tux pocket and wrote on the pad. He held it out. "I'll give you that."

JB looked at the number. "If you'll sign that, I'll see you in the suite. Eleven-thirty-ish?"

"And bring your brilliant wit." Christopher scribbled his name, handed over the paper, then huffily turned on his heel and left.

"That's what you pay me for," JB shouted after him.

JB folded the paper with the amount written on it and put it in his pocket. Perhaps a play after all, he was thinking. Or a new novel. Now that he was taken care of for the next year he could decide what he wanted to work on next at his leisure. Maybe another mystery?

The way Christopher had left the room JB could tell it was going to be an uncomfortable first few minutes at the meeting later. But he figured he could handle a bit of hostility. Christopher had also probably gotten the idea that the "arrangement" he'd alluded to was now at an end.

Len, his make-up finished, had turned on his chair and was watching JB.

"That's what I call negotiating," he said. "So, what has you hanging here?"

"Well, I wanted to talk..."

A boy stuck his head in the door. "Five minutes, Mr. Matthews."

"Right, Fred. Can it wait, JB? I have to be on stage."

"Of course."

◈ ◈ ◈

The consensus of the audience as gleaned by JB while he mingled with them in the lobby after the show, was they had a hit. Lee was a revelation. Betty a wonder, cavorting like that at her age. Len was marvelous. The new song charming, and the vaudeville farce that carried it a gem of Teddy's choreography.

But it looked like there was a problem or two. The show had run long. That always happened.

"Well, I thought it dragged getting to the finale...", one patron said.

JB moved to another group.

"It sure does need to move in the middle of that last act..."

And another voice.

"I like the new song. But its over so quick. It's more like a thought than a song..."

JB went to the meeting with an idea of how to fix the lag in the last act.

The pastrami was fatty.

Twenty

After his all night session working on the script of *Mrs. MacKenzie*, JB arrived back at his building close to four in the morning. He went straight up the stairs to Len's apartment on the floor above.

The expected writing session with only Christopher and JB had turned out to be more a meeting between the producers and the director with JB as a side dish. When JB got there they were all standing around the hotel room, drinks in hand, wanting assurances that they had a hit on their hands—or if there was a problem how was Christopher going to make it better?

Poor Christopher had been the object of their questioning for the previous half-hour. They had unilaterally come to the conclusion that there was something wrong in the third act, but had no idea what it was.

It had been easy enough for JB to point out the lag to them.

Dance: Ten

"Great," Christopher said. You could see it in his expression. His rescue was at hand. "How do we fix it?" The attention of the entire room turned to JB. He felt every eye watching him, waiting for his answer.

"Well, what if..." He suggested a reprise of the romantic ballad from act one. Give the audience a second helping of what had turned out to be a strong song for stating the characters opposite views on love. She was for it, he was agin' it. Having a second run of the song and switching the verses would signal their growth and newly discovered love for each other, bringing the two leads back together for a happy ending.

The idea was mulled over and then greeted with slaps on the back.

"I knew you were worth what we're paying you." Leave it to Christopher. He had taken JB's surprise negotiation and turned it around to make himself look better for the backers. The man could spin a hippo. Of course, with all the backers now knowing that it was JB who had saved the day, he was sure his name would make the rounds of all the other producers on the street. Soon the whole theater community would know and JB would have developed a reputation among the people who counted. A show doctoring career was launched.

🌑🌑🌑

Once the idea of how to fix the show was outlined JB then had to sit down and do the writing that would make it workable. He had to take the two leads into singing again for their happy ending. A transition like that could be tricky. If it was too abrupt it would be awkward. If it was over prepared with rococo underscoring it would be too predictable. JB also had to shift a scene and take out another to make the jump into the vaudeville finale smoother. To make it all work better, to tighten it. With that done JB felt he had earned his bump in salary.

The producer posse had left after the initial discussion. JB and Christopher were left to work out the changes on their own. It had been accomplished with civility by Christopher and JB focusing on the work. Getting the outline together had gone smoothly enough, although JB knew that further tightening might be needed. That was something Christopher would have to accomplish through both playing and rehearsing over the next few days.

JB had been up all night, using soda and sugar as a stimulant, writing the necessary dialogue for the new scenes. Christopher, on the other hand, had flaked out soon after the outline was finished. He stretched out on the couch and slept while JB wrote. It had been early in the morning when JB shook Christopher awake to tell him the work was done.

They discussed what the changes had accomplished, then JB told the director that he needed to talk about something personal with him.

"You don't want to see me anymore. That's it isn't it, JB? I kind of figured that out earlier."

"Actually, Christopher, we need to talk about your dating both Ms. Fairfax-Warner and me. I don't know if it's the right thing to do. Which of us are you cheating on?"

"Since there is no exclusive arrangement between any of us I don't get your question."

What was it Len had said about apples and trees? In this case it looked like Christopher was taking a branch from his father's tree after all. "In that case, maybe I should better ask how many are you presently seeing? How many men? How many women?"

"I don't see that its any of your business, JB. I see as many people as I want." Yep, same tree.

"Okay. That is your right I guess. I have no special claim on you. Nor, it appears, does your girlfriend. But it is my right to not put myself in jeopardy because of your promiscuity. And you shouldn't put anyone else in the same position."

"You mean AIDS, right? Well, I'm fine if that's what you're worried about."

"It is what I worry about. I know people that have become sick even when they hadn't had sex with anyone for ages. The disease seems to take a long time to show symptoms. You can't know if you're well or not. Have you been tested?"

"I didn't think I needed to. But maybe I should. I'll see my doctor. Soon."

"Please do. And do some serious thinking about which side of the fence you want to graze on. In this day and age its smart to start thinking about monogamy as a lifestyle. Do you want to spend your time with a man or a woman? A choice needs to be made. I can guarantee you'll be happier if you do."

That conversation done JB then executed one of the clauses in his new contract. He told Christopher he would be out of town for the next three days. Out of reach. After a bit of fluffel from Christopher it was agred JB would leave an emergency number when he had one. Wherever he was going.

They finally called it a night soon after three AM. JB found a cab in front of the hotel and directed it to East Sixty-fourth and Second Ave.

◈ ◈ ◈

Once back at the apartment he aimed straight up the stairs for Len's. The situation between Len and Jimmy Jameson had been at the back of his mind all evening. He didn't care if he woke Len at—what was it? Almost four—he had to explain what they had found out about Jimmy to cause him to be arrested on opening night.

He rang the bell and then knocked. He noticed his fist was shaking. To much sugar and caffeine from too much cola, he guessed. A sleepy Len, wearing an untied robe and pajama bottoms, opened the door a crack.

"Len, I'm sorry. I know its early, but I need to speak to you."

One of Len's eyelids opened a trembling eighth of an inch. The other remained closed. "Who are you?" Len mumbled.

"Len, wake up. It's JB. I need to talk with you."

"What time is it?"

"Three-fifty-seven."

"I got in twenty minutes ago. Coffee. I must have coffee."

"Let me in. I'll brew some."

"Bless you, strange visitor." He flung open the door. "Enter and prepare."

Len turned and stumbled over to the kitchen table. The fold-away bed was out, the blanket in a pile in the center. JB went to the sink in the efficiency kitchen and started making the promised liquid. Water in a kettle. Clean cups. Spooned crystals. Once the water was heating, JB sat across from Len at the table.

"Now, why have you woke me up, JB?"

"I wanted to talk to you about Jimmy."

He sighed. "I heard he got arrested. It was all over backstage tonight. But the person I got it from didn't know the reason. You do, I presume?"

"As a matter of fact I do. The police did a background check on your friend. They came up with another Jimmy Jameson. The real Jimmy Jameson. That Jimmy Jameson is a retired Broadway dancer who is currently the owner of a his own dance studio in Rochester, New York. That's upstate from here."

"I'm aware of that. He has the same name?"

"No, Len, he's the genuine article. The person you know here as Jimmy Jameson turns out to be a con-artist who stole the real Jimmy's credit card and identification two years ago. The Jimmy you know here lived with the real Jimmy for a years worth of dance lessons under the name Tommy Haines. He was Jimmy's lover. Then, after getting what he wanted, he disappeared, taking the real Jimmy's name, credit card, and as much as the ATM at the bus station would allow the guy to steal. After that the real Jimmy did some checking and found out that the fake Jimmy had done the same thing to a long series of men before him. He was using stolen identities with all of them. The guy would take their names and use them to become someone new."

"Your kidding."

JB was up now, pacing back and forth in front of the table.

"Good God, JB, what's got you so hyper? Are you on something? And whatever it is can you get it over the counter?"

"Sugar and caffeine, Len. That's all."

Len reached over and pulled JB's cup toward him. "Well, no more of this for you."

JB didn't pay attention. His mind was spinning too fast. He stopped pacing and faced Len. "I have to ask, did you give Jimmy any money? Because he was running a scam on you."

"No, of course not. First I offered to give him the cane I told you about. It's worth very near what he needed. But, Jimmy couldn't wait for an auction. He had to sign a lease and leave a deposit. So, I offered to match any funds he came up with in the next two weeks. That way we would be equal partners in the business. I'm not an idiot, JB."

"I have a feeling that maybe the cane is part of his scam, Len. I bet you its not worth anything."

"You know, I wondered about that. I don't remember seeing the initials that I was shown. I mean I carried that cane every night for a year and I'd never seen them. And what sort of actor would make them so small? Booth would have made those letters as big as his own ego. He wouldn't have settled for the tiny markings the doctor showed me."

"Doctor?"

"The expert Jimmy took the cane to. He has a shop on Madison. Is he a fake too?"

"Could be. It would fit in with a scam artist's modus operandi. He'd need someone to convince you that you had something valuable. Then you wouldn't think so much about giving away such a large amount of money."

Len shook his head. "So Jimmy was a certified con-man, huh?" JB nodded. "I had a feeling something wasn't right about him. I guess I slithered away from the snake this time. The field mouse is grateful for your intervention."

"Then you weren't emotionally involved with Jimmy. I was worried it would upset you. That's a relief."

"We were involved, and aren't you the coy one. Emotionally involved? We did get it on once, but not at all lately. We'd crossed over to just being friends. And, he seemed like he might have been a pretty good antiques dealer. I saw some of his finds and they were solid. And he'd found out that cane I had was worth some money, if it really is what he said it is?"

"What finds?"

"He showed me a storeroom full of antiques he'd bought over the years. Over on the West Side, near the old Coliseum. Why? You think they're stolen?"

"Who knows? It could be stolen goods. The police probably would be interested." JB got up from the table and went to the phone. "I'll leave a message for Kelly. He can check it out."

"Or, you and I could go over there and see for ourselves. How do you feel about going out for breakfast?"

JB hung up the phone. "Too late. The night officer took the message."

"Does that mean I don't get breakfast?"

JB and Len were huddled together inside the vestibule of the same storage building Len had been brought to a few nights earlier.

Looking through a pane of glass into the security office, JB was asking the guard inside if he could have the name of the owner of the storage unit Len had described to him.

The guard was saying it was privileged information, when Len leaned over JB's shoulder and said, "That isn't the guard I saw before. He's a different one."

JB started to ask, "Are you just starting your shift?", when Len interrupted.

"JB, there. At the door inside. That's the guy that was on the night I was here."

JB looked through the office window to the door. Standing in the doorway was a man of about thirty—the night man. Blond, seemingly clueless, he was in the process of slowly realizing he was the object of notice when Len began pointing at him. He couldn't have heard what was being said, not through the glass, but he was sure they were looking at him for some reason. When he recognized the man doing the pointing from the other night he decided to leave.

Len was shouting at the guard on duty to go get that guy so they could ask him some questions. JB was also shouting for him to tell him where the man would come out, since it was obvious he was running.

The guard pointed to the outside and JB took off out the door. When he stepped out on the street he looked to his left and saw the guy emerge from a door a few feet up from where he was standing. The man looked both ways and then turned to walk swiftly away toward the Avenue.

JB took off after him. His purpose was to catch up and ask him a couple of questions about the storage room. He didn't think about how aggressive it must have looked. As JB was about to come up along side the guy he raised his hand to get his attention. As JB did that the man reached into the pocket of his jacket, then halted and turned toward JB. He was holding a gun. A small gun, to be sure, but enough to do some damage. He pointed it at JB.

JB raised his arms and backpedaled a step or two, "Hey. Not at all necessary. I just wanted to ask a couple of questions."

The man spread his legs, planted his feet, adjusted his aim. "About what?"

"My friend,..." JB said, indicating Len who was coming up beside them. "...was shown a storeroom at the place where you work. That was about a week ago. You remember?"

The man nodded. Reluctantly.

"Could you tell us who rents that storeroom?"

Len huffed, "It was room six A. I remember that."

The man relaxed a bit and let the gun drop to his side. "That's the last room on the first floor. It belongs to the Whitney's. Family heirlooms."

"Then why was Jimmy Jameson showing those rooms as his own?"

The man lifted his hand, again pointing the gun at JB and Len.

"Now, really sir, you don't want to go waving that thing around like that. You could get into trouble."

"I could get in trouble if I answer your question."

Another voice chimed in, from behind the man.

"You're already in trouble for assault with an almost deadly weapon." Kelly poked his own gun into the back of the man. "Now, drop it before I have to do something drastic."

The guy dropped the gun. It clattered when it hit the concrete sidewalk. JB leaned forward and gingerly picked it up. He held it to his face and checked the chambers.

"Its not loaded, Kelly."

He handed it over to the cop.

Kelly took it after he had the man handcuffed and properly subdued.

"Not so deadly then," he said. "Still the threat was there."

"Charge him with conspiracy to be bitchy," Len suggested.

"Is this the guy you were going to talk too. I got your message."

"That's the one. I had just asked him why Jimmy Jameson was showing somebody else's property as his own when you came to our rescue."

"Well, answer the man."

"It was a joke. That's all. Jimmy said he was going to impress some guy with what he owned. As a joke."

"How much did he pay you?"

"Two hundred."

"Was it worth two hundred to lose your job and end up in police custody? You work cheap, mister."

Len said, "Uh, Lieutenant, I think this man was an accomplice of Jimmy's. I recognize that voice. He was the doctor. The man who authenticated my cane." Len pointed at him. "You were the doctor weren't you? Admit it."

"I don't know what your talking about."

"Sure you do. You put on a phony wig and a phonier accent and played the owner of the antique shop Jimmy took me to. So the cane is a fake, isn't it?"

Kelly pushed his gun into the man's back. "Tell us, mister. Or you might not make it back to the station."

"What? You can't do that. Not in front of witnesses."

JB chuckled. "What witnesses? I wasn't anywhere near here this morning. Were you, Len?"

"Okay, it was me. I've been helping Jimmy all along. We put the initials on the cane ourselves. But it was Jimmy's idea. I just went along with it."

"What about the ledger page?" Len asked.

"We showed you a copy. We faked the entry and pasted it over another entry from the ledger. A copy of that doctored document and you were none the wiser. It was easy."

"That's it. You're charged with intention to defraud. Now, come on..." Kelly grabbed a handful of the man's coat and started pushing him down the street.

# Twenty One

◈◈◈◈◈◈◈◈◈◈◈◈◈ There's
nothing like having a gun pointed at you to make one realize
how tired a person can be. The initial adrenaline rush at
the danger of it will push you up at first, but JB soon found
that you crash very fast. And then fatigue sets in.

Len had decided to stay on the West Side for the
promised breakfast they had been over there to have. It
would make it easier to get to the theater for rehearsal he
said. And he could always grab a few winks in his dressing
room. JB had elected to take a cab back home. He managed
to make it there that morning before he completely crashed.
Then he slept for six solid hours.

That's why Len wasn't aware that when JB woke he
bathed, dressed, packed, and walked to the local rent-a-
car office. There he took the cheapest sized car available,

refused the insurance, and drove it out of Manhattan, headed for Long Island.

◈ ◈ ◈

The town of Mawahawken was, to say the least, bleak. That was only one of the words JB could have used to describe the accumulation of buildings he found as he drove along the road leading into town. Dismal and forlorn also came to mind. Grey clapboard weathered looking houses lined cold uninviting streets. They led to a stone beach that was lapped at by uninspired sickly green waves. JB could understand why Ronald Prescott would have wanted to get out.

Facing the beach front was an early twenties built hotel. Designed in the Victorian gingerbread style popular then for resorts it was now peeling its once white paint and gap-toothed with missing geegaws and trims on the porch that spanned along the front. Rockers turned on their sides waited for guests that were apparently uninterested in watching a melancholy overcast afternoon.

JB parked in the hotel's side lot and made his way inside. The lobby, decorated in the same old-time splendor as the building lacked either warmth or hospitality. A man who looked as if he had been pulled from the grave stood impassively behind the desk. He wore a yellowed white shirt with a detachable collar and his sleeves had garters. A celluloid green shade covered his obviously myopic eyes as the glasses perched on his longish nose were bottle thick. He resembled something posing in Grandma's tintype album.

"I'd like a room, please."

"For overnight?"

"For a few days."

"That would be twenty-five a day. Winter rate."

"Fine."

"In advance."

"Sure."

JB handed over his card and waited while the man ran it. He went over to a rack of brochures and began looking through them. The place during the summer months looked to be lively with band concerts and ice cream socials, tea-dances and poetry readings. Now, in December, it was shuttered and frigid.

As was the room when he got in it. He pulled open the drapes and looked around. Rather plain, with a ghastly period flowered paper on the wall. The painted iron bed with a cotton crazy quilt was also out of the time before the stock market crash. A small color TV hidden in a fifties television cabinet was the only relief from the original old fashioned decor. He checked the steam radiator. It was cold. Turning the knob released a steady hiss as moist heat filled the room.

The bed turned out to be, after some misgivings as to its sturdiness, quite comfortable. JB was lulled to sleep by the drone of the TV and his exhaustion from the drive. But not before he kept his promise to Christopher and called long distance to leave the hotel phone number with his assistant. Then he closed his eyes and was out.

He woke at two-thirty AM, pee'ed, turned off the TV, by then playing static, and went back to sleep. When he next awoke it was nearly noon.

Rested, his stomach called out, so he showered and dressed quickly. Inquiring of the desk clerk where he might find a diner, the man literally spoke to the wall of mail cubbies rather than turn around and acknowledge JB's presence. He answered, snootily, that there was a luncheonette two doors down on Seaside. Seaside being the street running in front of the hotel. JB ignored the snub, putting it down to animosities between natives and out-of-towners—that sort of thing happened a lot. Townies usually hated the tourists that took over their homes every year. Provincetown, Woodstock, even Nantucket or the Hamptons were perfect examples of the phenomenon.

JB went outside. A grey overcast day, silver clouds rolled across the sky. It was nonetheless bright, the sun burning a hole through the haze. He turned and took in the town. It wasn't much. Rows of shops facing each other across a brick laid street.

The street was, like the hotel, a time capsule of the twenties, when it appeared the place had been established. There were wooden sidewalks with painted storefronts cloyingly called Shoppe's. Black painted iron posted lamps dotted the curbs. The main drag consisted of the hotel, a department store—the front window held a naked mannequin standing with its back to the world—a repair shop, two art galleries, a gaggle of antique shops and the luncheonette. That was all of beautiful downtown Mawahawken. Two streets, First and Second, crisscrossing Seaside was the main access to the rest of the town.

JB got his lunch. The waitress was a seventeen year old who tended to giggle even when he only said hello. While he downed a glass of water, he was thinking about where he might start his research into the true identity of Teddy Brewster. And if Ronald Prescott fit into the picture. He took the advice he usually found to be most helpful in these situations. He asked the girl where the local library could be found.

He turned his car onto First, drove through a neighborhood made up, close to the main street, of little woebegone cottages with limp banners and empty window boxes hanging off frost covered windows. These were the rentals the townies made their livings from. New Yorkers were willing to pay exorbitant prices for a two week rental during the months of June through to the last week of September. JB drove on. The landscape changed to more common houses and apartment buildings. Four stop lights down JB took a left and half way down on the right was the Mawahawken Public Library.

This was a Carnegie type building with two columns over a set of bronze doors. They held up a portico with a sculpture of Athena lying back reading a book while surrounded by cherubs. The place was no bigger than an average family house but overwhelming in its overdone decoration. JB climbed the granite steps by using the brass hand rail. Useful since the planning of the stone steps didn't consider the effects of cold weather on their surface. Damn things were icey, and slippery as hell.

Once inside he was stopped dead, carried back to his childhood by the smells and the ambiance of the small library. The stacks of books gave off a musty odor that was directly related to visits with his mother at a tender age. He remembered being deposited in the children's area and wondering at the wealth and fantasy he had found there. The library was always his refruge, his escape. It was where he discovered a wide and varied world outside of his small Kansas town, where he found inspiration and direction. It was a wonderous smell and he felt a shiver at its bouquet.

He went directly to the information desk and spoke with the librarian. Using his inside voice, he asked if they had copies of newspapers going back to the Nineteen-fifties. The woman, maybe a year or two older than JB, told him that they didn't keep big city papers, but did have the local paper in bound editions back to when the town was founded. It had flourished immediately then as a refuge from the city heat and had survived by serving the tourist trade. Also there was a small private college just thirty miles away, a rock quarry that had petered out in the Seventies, and during the Forties the area around the lake had become an enclave of rich people's summer homes.

The newspapers were kept in waist high bound copies along a shelf that reeked of dust and allergies. Each book contained ten years. That was five-hundred and twenty pages per book since the Mawahawken Sentinel was a weekly. The year Nineteen-fifty-two was placed on a table. Still standing, JB thumbed through the coverage of the murder trial of Theodore Brewinski.

Finally, under a headline, JB found a grainy black and white picture of the boy. Using a lighted magnifier he had found at the MOMA gift store he got in close on the face. The kid was only twenty when the photo was made. The Teddy JB knew was the public face. The one everybody saw when he was as famous as his work. Sparkling intense eyes, a Van Dyke beard, blow-dried thinning hair. Could this callow youth in a thirty-five year old picture have become Teddy Brewster? How the hell was he going to find that out?

He continued to flip through the pages of the paper. There was another picture of Theodore sitting at the defendant's table, behind him the faces of some of the spectators were visible. There was one face in the crowd that struck JB as familiar. Again with the magnifier. It was Ronald Prescott. Next to him was another boy. Black, skinny, looked to be the same age as Ronald. So Ronald had known Theodore before he arrived in New York.

The librarian leaned over and asked if he was finding

what he needed. He smiled and said yes. Then he asked her if she had known Theodore when she was younger.

"I should have known you would be reading about our famous murder, Mr. Bent." She reminded JB of Ernestine, the character Lily Tomlin had played on *Laugh-In*. "Oh, yes sir. I recognized you the minute you walked in. I've read all of your books, Mr. Bent. I just love them."

"Well, thank you."

"What are you looking for? The boy was acquitted. And he disappeared. Some people think it was a ghost or an alien that took him. I think he was killed. Is that why you're interested?"

"By who?"

"Oh, I think it was the other two robbers. He never gave their names but still it was those two that killed him after the trial. To make sure he'd never tell anyone. There's bones at the bottom of the lake if anybody cared to dredge it."

"Did you know the boy. You're about the right age."

"No, he was younger. The class behind me. And he was from Outer Mawahawken. We called that area out there the Wolf's Track, cause the wolves were always at the doors of the people who lived there. It was the poor side of town." She reached out and pointed to the picture of Theodore at the table, with the people behind him. She put her finger on one of the boys in the crowd. "But I knew him. And he knew Theo."

"Who is that?"

"Ronnie. Ronnie Prescott. He was my boyfriend for a little while. Until he went off to college. Now he's one of our most famous natives. He's a big shot on Broadway."

"Yes. I've heard of him. Tell me about him."

"For one of your books?" JB nodded. "Really? What do you want to know?"

"What kind of kid was he."

"Rich. Spoiled. And a hell-raiser." She pointed again at the paper. "The guy next to him was his best friend. Lionel. Really he was Ronnie's toady. Followed him everywhere."

"You said Ronnie knew Theodore?"

"Oh, of course. We all knew of him. It was a small town back then, Mr. Bent. But Theo wasn't part of the cool crowd. Ronnie, however, decided he liked Theo and let him hang around with him. Most of the rich kids wouldn't have any thing to do with a kid from the Wolf's Track. Ronnie was his friend up until Theo got arrested. Then he dropped him. Like all of us did. Theo was a criminal. Our parents would have freaked if we had helped him. I wish I hadn't given into that. I guess he could have used a friend then."

"Well, thank you again. You've been very helpful. By the way, do you know if any of Theo's relatives are still in town?"

"His sister is still here. Still out in the Wolf's Track. I'll get you her name and address."

JB waited while she went to the desk. She returned and slipped a *Post-it* in front of him. "Aren't we popular today? Another man just came in looking for the same papers you've been reading."

"Oh, who's that?"

"I have no idea. He was a stranger. Not a regular in the library anyway. He just asked if he could see the same newspapers you were looking at."

"I wonder why? He asked specifically to see what I was reading?" She nodded. "Is he still here? Where is he?" She pointed toward the desk. JB walked toward the front with the librarian following. The front was empty. No one else was in the building.

"He must have left. Funny, huh? By the way, I have Ronnie Prescott's mother's address too. She has a house over in Lakeview." She handed over another *Post-it*.

Dance: Ten

Twenty Two

So, they have a lake here. This close to the ocean? JB drove out to it. He went on First for about five miles, then he veered right to be in a, to say the least, more than affluent area. Two story fake English Tutor, High Victorian, or Cape Cod style houses abounded. Prime real estate being located right against the lake, which was, it appeared, just for show. It was stagnate and clogged with reeds. Colored an unhealthy green with frozen patches around the edges it was probably man-made, fed by a stream meant to run into the nearby ocean that was dammed at one end. He turned onto Lake Drive. It seemed a safe bet that was where he would find Ronald Prescott's mother. Still living. She must be in her seventies.

Dance: Ten

JB found the address and turned into the pebble covered driveway's half circle. This was one of the faux Tutor style homes, but only in its lines. The building materials were entirely of wood, not the usual stucco. Clapboard siding, darker stained wood to highlight the windows and door frames. There was a black wreath hanging on the front door.

Of course, Mrs. Prescott would have been notified of Ronald's death by now.

JB used the bell and waited. The door was opened by an elegant man approaching his fifties, dressed in a finely tailored Brooks Brothers suit, with a red tie. "Yes, sir," he sniffed. JB was dressed casually so he probably had mistook him for a tradesman or delivery man.

"Hello. Is the lady of the house available. I know its unlikely under these circumstances." He indicated the wreath. "But perhaps she'll see me."

The man at the door nodded, but then said, "Mrs. Prescott is not here. She has gone to New York to retrieve her son's remains." He reached out and adjusted a leaf on the wreath. "But if you have something for her...? Or you can leave your name? I will tell her you called."

"Then you would be her...."

"Personal Assistant. Osgood Millington. And for a good many years I've held the position. Now, if you will excuse me I have the funeral arrangements to make for her. It will be a small ceremony."

"Are you sure? Wasn't Ronald Prescott a famous person here in Mawahawken. That should bring the mourners out."

"I hadn't considered that. Humm, perhaps I should take that under advisement. Now, what was it you were seeking of Mrs. Prescott."

"Oh, my name is Jeremy Bent. I'm a writer. I'm doing research on a book I'm working on. About Teddy Brewster. The dancer. I'm interested in a murder trial that went on here in the fifties. I understand Ronald was a friend of the defendant in that trial. Theodore Brewinski. Maybe you were around then. Do you remember him?"

Osgood looked about, first one way then the other. Then he looked JB up and down. There was a subtle shift in his manner as he said, "Why don't we go inside. It's too chilly out here to be talking. My office is just there, down the hall."

JB followed the gentleman into the house. His office was dark wood with a heavy mahogany desk. JB took the overstuffed armed chair in front of the desk.

"I was in Mrs. Prescott's employ during that time. Master Ronnie was quite a handful back then. Young, just past being a teenager. Prone to visits from the Sheriff. Petty things. When his mother finally had enough she issued an ultimatum. He would stop his shenanigans or be cut from the will. Well, for some obscure reason, he did exactly that. He picked up, straightened himself out, and ended up making a success of himself in New York. His reformation was quite sudden. Almost overnight. We were quite shocked at the time."

"Ronald Prescott never struck me as the rebellious type. More Wally Cox than James Dean." JB smiled at Osgood.

Then again Wally Cox was part of the Marlon Brando gang, wasn't he?, JB thought to himself. He rode motorcycles. Wore leather jackets. The whole Hell's Angel's schemer. Maybe Prescott could have been a bad ass kid. "What kind of mischief did he get into," JB asked.

"Master Ronnie was a spoiled young man who had far too much money and not enough ambition. When his mother threatened him it didn't even matter to him. He had his own money from his paternal grandmother. A yearly trust. He didn't care if he was cut out of anybody's will. That was what made the change in Ronald all the more surprising. The belligerence dropped away in an instant. Diligence replaced sloth."

"When was this miraculous change?"

"In Nineteen-fifty-two. In fact, right after the trial of that boy you asked about. That Theo Brewinski. When he got off Ronnie was very upset about it. Although, I myself was of the opinion that the verdict was a fair one. When they handed down the not guilty verdict Ronnie stood up and stomped out of the courthouse. Then he simply disappeared for a day or two. He showed up finally, but he was different from then on. More adult. Like he had taken on some burden that weighed upon him. Then that young man, Theo, he up and disappeared. Just left town. Like Ichabod Crane."

"I doubt there's any headless horsemen on Long Island."

"Probably not."

"So Ronnie changed…"

"Completely. He went off to college and never really returned home again. Then he dropped out of school after six months and went off to the big city. Where he did quite well it appears. It was a damaged relationship between mother and son for a very long time. They hadn't seen each other for years, and now we get word of his death." Osgood shook his head. "You know, Ronald didn't even stop at this house the last time he was in town."

"When was that?"

"Oh, several years ago. A year or so after the trial, if I remember correctly. He was here for the funeral of one of his high school friends. Lionel Huttelson. They were quite close in school. Lionel was Ronnie's hanger on. That boy was willing to do anything for Ronnie. He totally idolized him. Personally, I think there was a bit more to it than that. What I think is Lionel was in love with Ronnie. And not in a healthy way. If you know what…." Osgood stopped, thought better of what he was saying, and changed gears mid-sentence. "Anyway, Lionel was killed in a car wreck. Out at the old quarry. Ronnie came to town then, attended the service, and left. Didn't even look in his mother's direction on his way out of town. And now she'll have to bury him."

"Shoot. I was hoping to talk to this kid Lionel. He was in that picture of the trial I saw in the papers. Sitting behind Theo. I sure would have liked to ask him a few things. There aren't many people who remember like you."

"Would Lionel's great-grandmother help you? She's still alive. She's over a hundred and lives over at the old folks home on Elm. Call her Miz Bittie, everybody does. You should speak with her. Or try the Sheriff. He could probably tell you about young Ronnie Prescott. They certainly had their run-ins at the time."

"I will." JB stood. "And thanks for your help."

Murder: Maybe?

◈◈◈

Osgood shut the front door on JB. He turned and headed for his car, then noticed another car parked out on the street. He noticed it because it was so out of place. A dented, pitted, wreak of a faded silver Chevy with a missing side view mirror. It definitely didn't belong in the upper class environs of the Lakeside neighborhood. Inside was a man sitting behind the wheel faining indifference while actually watching JB's every move.

When JB pulled away the man in the silver Chevy started up and followed. JB drove back to the main road and turned back toward town. The silver car with that missing mirror did the same.

JB stopped at a gas station, filled up, got directions for the home where this Miz Bittie lived, and headed for Elm Street. He figured that if there was a one-hundred-and-one year old woman sitting in a rocker he had better get there soon. She could croak from a hardy sneeze. He wasn't sure what he expected to get from the old woman but he was trying to fill in the blanks in this whole thirty year old tale. There were things that weren't being said. He knew he wasn't getting the whole story. He felt it. Maybe what this Miz Bittie knew about Lionel would fill in the blanks. Interesting that this was a black kid hanging around with a white kid on Nineteen-fifties Long Island. There probably weren't many Negroes in Mawahawken in those days. And this one black kid was running with one of the richest kids in town. That must have irked a few of the natives when you consider the prevailing attitudes in that pre-civil rights era.

◈◈◈

The rest home was a fairly modern Nineteen-seventies type of facility. It looked not so much like an adult care residence as a motel out on the highway. Ranch style, all on one floor, it meandered off in two directions from a central building that housed the office, dining room, and other facilities.

JB went to the lobby desk and inquired after a Miz Bittie. Could he talk with her? The young woman there directed him to the day room, saying he would find her in there with her nurse attendant.

175

Looking in he saw a tiny woman sitting in a wheelchair by a bank of potted plants. And she was as advertised. Old. He bet her liver spots had liver spots. She was a little wizened thing wrapped in a pale pink quilted robe. Her head was almost lost in the folds it made around her narrow shoulders. There was a cotton candy fluff of white hair. Her skin was a charcoal grey and deeply wrinkled. Her jaw was going up and down in a constant chewing motion, as if her lips were on the menu for lunch. JB was reminded of the scene in *Lost Horizon* when Margo was carried out of Shangri-La.

Sitting next to her, quietly reading a magazine, was a younger woman. In her forties. From the uniform she wore she had to be the nurse the receptionist had mentioned. JB walked over to her and said, "Hello. I was wondering if I could speak with her?" He indicated the old lady.

"What for?" the nurse asked protectively.

JB again used his book story and after some consideration the nurse said it would be all right. JB sat next to her and gently reached out to touch the old woman's hand, mostly to get her attention, as she seemed to be off somewhere in her own memory. The hand was dry parchment stretched over thin brittle bone. She lifted her head and focused rummy eyes on him. Then mumbled something incoherent.

The nurse said, "She want's to know what you want? She's kinda hard to understand when she talks, so I'll tell you what she say's. Is that okay?"

"That would be fine. Miz Bittie, I'd like to ask you about your great-grandson, Lionel?"

The old woman again began to mutter, while the nurse translated. JB sat quietly and let her go on. He would ask an occasional question but mostly the old lady rambled and mumped, eventually giving him the pertinent information he could place in the scheme of the story he was seeking.

"Lionel's been gone more than thirty years now," she said. "Outlived them all I did. More's the shame. Ain't right a mother should outlive her children. Lionel, he was a good boy. A bit queer like, maybe, but a real nice boy. Got mixed up with that rich kid though. That's what sent him wrong." She stopped and ruminated a bit then began to mutter again. "I never believed that his brakes failed and he crashed into that quarry. Balderdash. The boy was an ace mechanic. He took care of that old Ford Fairlane of his like it was his own child. No way he would have had bad brakes. The boy was killed, I jest know it. The damn state police would never look into it though. Poor boy, should have never got mixed up with them folks from out at the lake. That boy led Lionel wrong, he did. Then they had a big fight and that was the end of him..."

JB asked what fight and when was it.

She continued as if she hadn't heard him. "Boy was mixed up in something bad. A grandmother knows. He wouldn't tell me what, but I knew. He had stuff he shouldn't have. Expensive things. We didn't have the money to buy that sort of stuff. Told me it was presents from that Ronnie boy, but I knew better. I did like watching that TV though. Milton Berle. Uncle Miltie." She snorted at her remembrance, then continued. "I knew those boys was robbing people. That's what was going on. I knew it. But I sure enjoyed watching that TV. Then some other boy here in town. Some other boy Lionel knew got caught shooting someone. Killed em' dead he did. Well, that pulled Lionel up and made him think. Gave him a real come-uppance, it did. He cleaned himself up after that. But that Ronnie boy, that rich kid, wouldn't let him go. Kept after him all the time. Until they had a big old argument a couple of years later. Right out on the front lawn, they were. Right in front of the neighbors. Shouting and almost punching at each other. Fighting like animals they were. And then, the very next day, Lionel was dead. Gone." She quieted down then. The nurse explained how she tired easily.

JB thanked her and watched as the nurse wheeled Miz Bittie back to her room.

Dance: Ten

Twenty Three

◆◆◆◆◆◆◆◆◆◆◆◆◆◆ Intending
to stop at the diner next to the hotel for lunch, JB got
in his car and started back toward downtown. It seemed
Mawahawken didn't rate a fast food place yet. Or, at least
one that was open. He had passed one on the road but it
was boarded up with a painted 'Closed For The Winter'
sign on its front.

The whirling red light and siren behind him startled
him in its insistence. He pulled over to the berm and waited
while the cop got out and walked to his car. An unzipped
down coat showed the officer's gold plated badge glinting
on his chest. The cop stopped at JB's window. He rolled it
down.

"Was I doing something wrong, Officer?"

The man leaned down to better see JB. He was a black man, somewhere in his sixties, or close to retirement at any rate, and looked as if he had gained some weight recently. His blue shirt was stretched across an expanse of pot belly potruding over the belt at his waist. White dusted his close cropped hair, deep lines creased and furrowed at his nose and forehead.

He said, in a voice James Earl Jones would envy, "Are you the gentleman that spoke with Miz Bittie just now?" JB nodded. "Then I was wondering if I could talk with you? Do you mind if I get in?"

He didn't wait for an answer, but instead started to walk around the car aiming for the passenger side.

JB sat and waited as the cop came around. A silver Chevy, with a missing side view mirror, passed by, the driver rubbernecking as he did. JB had spotted the car before. First at Mrs. Prescott's and then in the parking lot of the old folks home he had just left.

The cop knocked on the side window and JB reached over to pull up the latch. He got in, removed his hat, and turned toward JB.

"Thank you, sir. I wanted to ask a couple of questions. Purely social. Do you mind?"

"No, of course not. What can I do for you, Sheriff?" Then remembering Osgood's advice he added, "As a matter of fact, I was hoping I could speak with you too."

"Yeah? Well, you go first then."

"Okay. I wanted to ask you about a young man who used to live here in town. A boy named Ronnie Prescott."

"When Miz Bittie's nurse called me, she mentioned you had asked about him. What was it you needed?"

"I've been given to understand that back when Ronnie lived here he was quite a handful. Is that right?"

"Why do you want to know? Don't get me wrong, I'm not trying to avoid giving you an answer, but I do want to know before I say anything."

JB once more wiped his book story clean and presented it to the Sheriff. The officer mulled it over a second and then nodded.

"I remember him. Now he lives up in your neck of the woods. You're from New York City, aren't you?"

JB nodded. "The Eastside forests and glens."

"Thought so. Could tell from your clothes. Barneys?"

"Bloomingdales, actually."

"I've lived here my whole life, but I get into the city every once in a while."

"And you've been a cop here for all that time?"

"Sure have. Started on the force back in Forty-seven. As a patrol cop. The only Negro on the force then. A pure-dee token I was. Now I'm the head man. Times has changed."

"You must have been one of the few blacks in the whole town then?"

"That's right. There were only about twelve families here then. We were all related in one way or another."

"Then the other boy, Lionel, was a relative?"

"My nephew. My brother married his mother. Miz Bittie's granddaughter. Lionel's mother. When my brother died of an heroin overdose in Forty-nine I sort of replaced him for Lionel. Then Lionel's mother went the next year. Same thing. I looked out for Lionel like he was my own after that."

"But he was dead just a year after that, according to Miz Bittie."

"That's right. Car crash out at the quarry. Brakes failed on the turn and he went over the edge. It was a shame. Lionel, if he'd got it together, was a real smart kid. He could have gone somewhere. Maybe even to college."

"Sorry."

"It was a long time ago. Why are you dredging all this up now?"

"As I said, for my book."

"On Teddy Brewster? Don't look so surprised. I know who he was. What I don't know is how he's involved with us here in Mawahawken."

"His partner and long time producer was Ronald Prescott. He was from here."

"True enough. But what's the connection?"

"Background for the book. Teddy's story has to include Ronald, so I need to fill in his past. You know that Ronald Prescott is dead, don't you Sheriff? He died of a heart attack just last week."

"No kidding? Well, that explains why Mrs. Prescott went

out of town then."

"What can you tell me about Ronald when he was living here. I've been told you and he had a few problems back then."

"More than a few. He was a bad kid. Always in trouble. And no reason for it. He had his own money. Lived out at the lake. He didn't need other people's things. He didn't need to be involved in those kinds of trouble."

"What kinds of trouble?"

"The kid was a sneak and a thief. He used to break into the summer houses around here. Caused all kinds of mischief. Stole stuff. Wreaked houses. Broke windows. Spray painted walls. That sort of thing. As I said, there was no reason for it either. I think it was a control thing for him. He had a sort of gang he ran."

"And Lionel was a part of that?"

"Yes he was. Part of the reason I was always after Ronnie. I wanted him to leave Lionel alone. But, Lionel followed Ronnie around like a lap dog. It was downright embarrassing to watch. I tried to get them apart but I couldn't. Lionel just did anything that arrogant little shit told him too. That other kid, Theo, he was the same way. I never did understand what power Ronnie held over them. It was pure-dee unnatural. That trial was what finally got them apart. When Theo was arrested they stayed away from him. And Ronald stopped seeing Lionel too."

"Except for this." JB handed over a copy of the newspaper picture showing the three boys at the trial. "They obviously were interested enough to go to Theo's trial. At least once."

"They was kids. Curiosity. Hell, the whole town was interested. "

"The courtroom was packed, huh? And, who can guess what goes on with kids and their hormone addled brains."

"True enough. But, you know, that Ronnie turned out to be okay. When he was growed up he turned out to be loyal to his friends. After Lionel died he used to send Miz Bittie money every month."

"Really?"

"Every month, like clockwork, five hundred dollars was deposited in her account at the bank. My brother-in-law worked there. He told me about it. Course it was just deposited from another bank. A bank in New York City. It had to have come from Ronald Prescott. He's the only one who could afford it. Nice of him, huh?"

Or was it some other reason?, JB was thinking. Like guilt maybe?

The Sheriff said, "So, that's why you came to town? To find out about Ronald Prescott?"

"That's for sure. I've already talked to Osgood Millington out at the Prescott house. And I've gotten interested in that murder trial too."

The cop snorted. "That old woman. Osgood is the biggest gossip in this whole town. But, he's right, you should look into that trial. It made Ronnie and Lionel take notice. They knew that if they kept on the way they was they'd end up the same way as that Theo kid. You should read the trial transcript. It's at the courthouse. If you want you can follow me there. I'll get Gert to pull it for you."

"That would be great. And how about I buy you lunch before we go. A deal?"

◆◆◆

A cheeseburger and fries served as lunch, then JB followed the Sheriff in his rental car over to the courthouse. They parked in a space out front and walked up the stone steps into the gold domed municipal building.

Upstairs in Records the Sheriff greeted Gert then talked for a moment with her. She disappeared and quickly returned with a folder of the requested trial transcript. The Sheriff handed it over to JB then excused himself to attend to his own business.

JB sat at a table similar to the ones used in the town library and began to read. Dry and uninteresting described most of the content, so JB took to skimming over the most boring parts. He slowed when he got to a part where a police officer was called to the stand to explain why the defendant on the first day of trial was wearing a swath of bandage on his head.

Defense Question: Officer Graham, can you tell us how Mr. Brewinski was injured?

Officer Answer: Yes sir. The prisoner, in the process of being apprehended, was running from the arresting officer. He had jumped from the vehicle

183

he was driving, abandoned it, and began an escape attempt. The apprehending officer, after pursuing the suspect, tackled him and brought him down. In the scuffle that followed the suspects head was rolled against a tree trunk. That was what was responsible for his injury.

Defense Question: I see, then the defendant was escaping and in the course of that attempt was injured.

Prosecution: Objection. Already stated.

Judge: Sustained. Move on Councilor.

JB also stopped skimming when Theo was called to the stand...

Defense Q: I want to return to the night Rosa Martinez was killed. Where were you when you heard the shot, Mr. Brewinski?

Brewinski A: I was sitting in the car with the motor running. The other guys were inside the Dean's house. In his study.

Defense Q: And what were you witness to from your position in the car?

Prosecution: Objection. Hearsay.

Defense Q: It goes to culpability your honor.

Judge: I'll allow it. Answer Mr. Brewinski.

Brewinski A: I was able to see through the picture window on the front of the house into the Dean's study. I heard the gun shot and then I saw a woman stumble backwards across the window. She clutched at her throat and held out a cross she had around her neck. Then she fell down. Straight down, like a sack on a rope at a hanging. She didn't get back up again.

Defense Q: And the two men inside. Did you see them?

Brewinski A: Not after I heard the shot. Before that I could see their flashlights sweeping in the dark of the room. Then the study lights came on. Real bright. It was like a movie screen. That must have been when the woman came in and found the two guys. After that I didn't see them again. They must have run out the back.

Defense Q: And what did you do when you saw this development?

Brewinski A: I was surprised. No one was supposed to have a gun. No one was supposed to get hurt. But I waited a few minutes to see if the guys were coming out. When they didn't I decided to take off.

Defense Q: And what happened then?

Brewinski A: I didn't even get back to the main road. The cops stopped me before I could.

Then the prosecutor had a go at him…

Prosecutor Q: Mr. Brewinski, all during this investigation you have refused to identify the two men who were with you that night.

Brewinski A: Yes, sir.

Prosecutor Q: Don't you think it might have gone easier on you if you had? These two men you allege were with you could have saved you from this trial completely.

Brewinski A: I suppose so.

Prosecutor Q: Isn't it true you were alone in that study that night? That it was you who killed Rosa Martinez in cold blood.

Defense Q: Objection. He's leading the witness.

Prosecutor Q: Withdraw the question. Well then, Mr. Brewinski, the two men who you claim were the perpetrators of this crime. Where might they have disappeared too?

Brewinski A: I don't know where they are. Like I said I never saw them come out of the study. They ran off and I haven't seen them since.

Prosecutor Q: And what makes you think we will believe these figments of your imagination, Mr. Brewinski?

Defense Q: Objection.

Judge: Sustained.

Brewinski A: No. You have to believe me. They were real. They really were there. I only met them a couple of hours before. In the quad. They tricked me. To help them with that stupid prank. That's what they said. I didn't know they were going to rob the Dean's house. I didn't even know they had a gun. I didn't do this. I swear.

Judge: Sustained. Councilor move on.

Prosecutor Q: We've heard all this before. No more questions.

Defense Q: Redirect, your honor?

Judge: Go ahead. But keep it brief. Lunch recess is approaching.

Defense Q: Mr. Brewinski, what is your real reason for refusing to identify the two men who were with you that night?

Brewinski A: I'm afraid for my life. Those guys already killed that poor woman. I don't want to be next. I won't finger them.

Defense Q: Even if you were protected?

Brewinski A: By who? The police? They already said they don't have the manpower. I'd be a sitting duck on the outside. I'll be dead before I leave the courthouse if I name them.

From there on the trial seemed to go Theo's way. His impassioned plea during his testimony managed to sway the jury into an acquittal. He was released, and disappeared within days. Never to be seen in Mawahawken, Long Island again. Some thought he was caught by the two men and, like Jimmy Hoffa, was buried in a landfill somewhere. Others thought he simply left town to start over. If Theo Brewinski was Teddy Brewster then JB knew the answer to the mystery. He knew where Theo had disappeared to. And, now, thirty-five years later he was really dead.

Twenty Four

As
JB left the courthouse, down in the parking spaces, he
spotted the silver Chevy. The one with the missing side view
mirror. It was conspicuously in JB's view. He sauntered over,
ever so nonchalantly, to stand in front of the automobile.
Imitating a goose pecking for food, he quickly ascertained
that it was empty. Going to the driver's side window, and
looking inside, he could see, displayed on the dashboard, a
stack of business cards for a private investigator. A real one
from the looks of the gold seal on the corner. Local from the
printed address.

Why was a PI on his tail? And not a very prosperous
one if the car was any indication. But how prosperous would
a private detective be in a town the size of Mawahawken?

"What are you looking in my car for?"

Dance: Ten

JB stood quickly. Standing on the sidewalk was a bruiser of a man. Ex-cop or ex-military. Strong jaw, muscled at one time now gone soft. Cheap suit, hard set mouth. "I'm sorry," JB said. "But that's a question I might better ask you. Why have you been following me all over town?"

"That's my business. Not yours."

"I think it is mine. What interest would a PI have in me?"

"What makes you think I'm a PI?" He stepped off the sidewalk and came right up to JB. Daring him to ask another question.

"The card on the dashboard for one. And you have the look."

"What look is that?"

"Down on his heels. Drinks too much. Shyster type."

"Why you…" The man pulled his arm back, folded his fingers into a fist and made ready to punch JB in the face.

As the fist came forward JB reached out with both hands, grabbed the swinging fist, and using some sort of physics equation he couldn't for the life of him explain, twisted as hard as he could, causing the bruiser to also twist. JB then leaned into the man's back and pushed, with the result that the bruisers arm went up behind his back as he fell forward onto the hood of his car.

"Now, tell me who hired you?" JB again pushed on the man's arm. He wriggled under him.

"I don't know. I only got a phone call hiring me to keep tabs on you while you were in town. That's all, mister. I don't even know who you are."

"You always go around getting into fights with strangers? That's not a very nice way to meet people." JB loosened his grip and the man stood. He faced JB as he rubbed at his arm.

"Was it a man or a woman who hired you?"

"A woman. But she didn't give me her real name. Said it was Smith. Unlikely."

"Well, I'll make your job easier. I'm going to make one more visit to one more person and then I'm leaving town. That's it. I get that I'm not welcome in your little burg."

◈ ◈ ◈

JB walked back to his own car.

Murder: Maybe?

If I'm being followed there is good reason to believe the PI had been hired by Mrs. Prescott, Robert's mother. Maybe I'm digging too deep for her comfort?

For whatever reason, JB had decided right then to make his visit to the sister of Theo Brewinski his last. Then he'd 'git to truckin' as the saying had it. It would put him back in New York City by evening, and it would mean good-by to Mawahawken. No great loss. So he drove to the hotel, packed, settled the bill, then checked for directions out to the Wolf's Track.

The road out to the Wolf's Track passed by rows of store fronts getting progressively shabbier the closer he got to this notoriously poor part of town. According to all he'd heard regenerated wasn't a word ever used to describe the area. Except for a pool of better kept buildings that surrounded the college campus the shabbiness of the place was unremitting. Once past the college grounds it instantly changed back to old and unused. Most of the stores in this part of town were boarded up with tattered For Rent signs tacked to their plywood covered doors.

Then he left the business district and houses began to dominate JB's route. This area was an eclectic mix of well kept or unkempt front yards and porches. JB found the street called Tearful Glen and understood completely why it had the appellation. The entire street was made up of run down houses or tin trailers attached to concrete foundations. The wooden houses had unpainted siding, hanging shutters, and overgrown yards. The trailers needed paint. Cars on cement blocks filled several of the yards. A chicken wire rabbit hutch filled one yard. A couple of the houses were obviously abandoned. The sister's house was in the middle of the street, on the right.

It wasn't quite as bad as its surroundings. A chain link fence with ivy twining through it surrounded the front yard. Inside was a wonderland of mosaic art pieces. The owner had taken shards of old china plates, teacups, reclaimed tiles, a bucket of cement and created art. Planters five feet tall, holding up art pottery basins, filled with hanging leafy plants. The walkway underfoot was likewise made of grouted plates and shards of tiles. JB followed it to an arched doorway also in the mosaic used everywhere else. A hobbyist with too much time on her hands?

He rang the bell and waited. Soon enough the door was opened and what looked to be a twelve year old girl answered.

"Hi, is your mother at home?" JB asked.

In a voice deepened by years of too many cigarettes, she said, "I'm the lady of the house."

She said this while peering from behind a thick pair of glasses, in heavy Buddy Holly type frames. The lenses had a thin film of gray powder covering them.

"What can I do for you?"

"I'm sorry. It was the pigtails." She wore braids on each side of her head. They were sticking out from under a blue western style handkerchief, tied babushka style. She had on a heavy canvas apron that hung to her knees, with black rain boots sticking out from under that.

"Let me introduce myself. My name is Jeremy Bent. I'm a writer, here doing research."

She cut him short. "Yeah. Yeah. Ethel, the librarian, called and said you might be coming by." She pulled off one of her heavy gardening type gloves. It was caked with a line of clay semi-dried and cracked as if it was a desert. "You want to talk about Theodore?" She huffed. "Tootsie Rolls, I haven't thought about him in years."

JB began to rethink his earier twelve year old assessment. Cursing had never been so mild.

"Come on in. We can jaw if you want." She turned and walked away.

JB stepped in.

The house was a total amazement. Even more so than the outside. The walls and twenty or so whatnot tables were lined with collectibles. Two tall glass cases filled with old dolls dressed in high Victorian splendor flanked a doorway. Laces and frills were in abundance. Hanging on the walls were puppets. Indian rod puppets. Asian shadow puppets. There was a Howdy Doody. And a Jimmy O'Day. The couch and chair were straight out of the Forties even to having white crocheted doilies on the velvet arms. The seats were covered in *Barbie* dolls, some still in the original boxes, their Bob Mackie wardrobes still glittering their Seventies' glamour. There was only a narrow ledge for actual seating.

In what should have been the dining room the woman's mosaic work had completely taken over the space. The kitchen was also piled high with collectibles, with at least five sets of dishes, each in a different pattern. Fiesta. Wedgewood. Plus as many sets of glasses. This woman has got to be stopped, JB was thinking.

"Take a seat." She indicated a dining chair with a crazy quilt cushion tied to the back and seat. She leaned back against the work table that stood behind her.

"She also said you were a famous writer. She didn't say you'd be so danged cute." And she fluttered her eyelashes at him. Was she flirting? Well, that has to be stopped, JB decided. She isn't going to collect me that's for damn sure.

"Obviously she also didn't mention what kind of books I write." He explained that he was gay and wrote gay themed mysteries. That led them to why he was interested in Theo. And to Ms. Brewinski telling JB that when Theo ran away, that was the last she had heard from him. "Never a word. Not even a card when my youngest passed away Nary a Christmas card either. He's been completely gone. To something better I hope."

"Then you don't believe he's dead."

"No sir I don't. I sense things, you see."

JB just bet she did...

"And I would know if he had passed over to the other side. Do you believe in reincarnation, Jeremy Bent."

"Call me JB. Everyone does. I believe in exactly what I'll find one second after I'm dead. It could just be dark and unaware over there, you know? I was wondering, is it possible that your brother, Theo, might have run away to New York, changed his name, and became someone named Teddy Brewster." She pulled her head back. "Have you heard of him?"

She shook here head no. JB explained who the famous dance director was to Broadway and in the movies. She reared her head back and laughed. It was a hearty laugh, the kind of laugh people use in a bar on a crowded Saturday night. "I'm sorry, but I was remembering Theo dancing to that *American Bandstand* show on the TV when he was a youngster. He was a stitch. All elbows and knees. I can't see him ever being a professional dancer. Although he was amazing at picking up dance steps. He'd see it once on the TV and he could do it better than them. He could do some smooth moves sure, but it was what you call eccentric dancing. Like that Buddy Epsen used to do in them old movies."

"Interesting. Elbows and knees were what made Teddy Brewster famous. What can you tell me about his youth? When you were children. What was he like?"

"Well, we were best of friends. Theo and I had this spooky connection. We were like twins. You know what twins are like?"

"They finish each others sentences."

"Well, Theo was like my doppelganger. A small replica of me. We had so much fun when we were little. Then he got older and he got secretive. Right when he started hanging around with that Ronnie kid. Theo was just a junior high school kid when Ronnie took a shine to him. The two of um hung out all through high school. Ronnie was the next class up from Theo. I was in the one before him. Then Theo got blamed for that murder. You'd better believe you didn't see hide nor hair of Ronnie then."

JB handed over the picture from the trial. "Well, they got together at least once."

"I remember this. That day a whole class of high school kids went to the trial. It was a carnival in the courthouse. Photographers and reporters all over. That day, at a break, one of the photographers got permission to take some pictures of Theo. The guy wanted a crowd behind him, so he recruited about a dozen kids to fill in the seats behind him. That must be why Ronnie is in this." She tapped on the photo. "Yep, sitting right next to him is Lionel. They were all three thick as thieves."

"Do you think Theo did it?"

"No, I don't. The Theo I grew up with wouldn't kill nobody. He was only the driver, remember. I'll bet he felt like he was watching a drive-in movie when he saw that lighted picture window. Talk about a horror movie. That would have beat *Frankenstein* all to hell."

"When was the last time you saw him."

"Right after the trial. He still had that ugly gash, all

stitched up on the front of his head. He was real agitated. Was pacing the house. He went out when a car honked for him. He was gone about thirty minutes. Then he came back, went straight to his room and started packing. He was out of here in less than an hour. He only stopped long enough to kiss me and give me two thousand dollars in cash. And you know what, about five years later someone started putting two hundred dollars in my bank every month. I figured it was some sort of insurance payout. Let me tell you it sure helps me get through the winters. Summers, I sell my mosaic's in a gallery here in town."

JB didn't have the heart to tell her that money would probably stop now. Would her mosaic's manage to make up the difference? They would have to, wouldn't they?

"What kind of car was it that honked for Theo that afternoon?" he asked.

"A Ford Fairlane. I remember because it was cherry apple red, with fifteen coats of lacquer. Lionel had shown it in the auto show the year before."

"So it was Lionel's car?"

"It probably was. Unlikely there'd be two in town. Though I didn't see who was driving it"

"And Lionel and Ronnie were always together?"

"Yep."

"Where do you think Theo got the two thousand dollars he left you?"

"Someone paid him to get out of town. I knew that. No one from this side of town had that kind of money. Not then."

"How did Theo really get the wound on his head?"

"He said it was the cops did it. When he wouldn't give them the names of the two boys that were with him they tried to beat it out of him. He was acting all funny because of it. All disoriented. And he kept complaining that he couldn't catch a breath. Because they broke his nose is why. He was blowing his nose all the time. Although I think some of that blowing was tears too. He was leaving everything he knew. And we both knew he couldn't come back here no more."

"Listen you said that all three of the boys were always together. Do you think that night at the Dean's house there weren't two college boys, but his two accomplices were Ronnie and Lionel. That would mean Theo lied on the stand?"

"To protect them."

"Absolutely."

"Wouldn't put it past him."

And that was why Ronald Prescott had a built in entré into show business when he left college. The same college that Theo was supposed to have been picked up at by two strangers. The same college he had passed on the way here.

JB thanked the lady and got back into his car. He drove the reverse of his trip out there. When he got to the entrance to the college he turned in. The campus was like going back in time to an English prep school of the Edwardian age. Mr. Chips territory. Wooden sign posts that were written in Old English script gave a theatrical direction to the campus. JB turned to the right and followed a tree lined street on a circle. The circle passed by the dean's house. The day was starting to dim so JB had some trouble reading mail boxes and signposts. Finally another cutesy sign identified the home of the Associate Dean for Higher Education.

The house sat back from the street, and was separated from the curb by a low hedge of boxwoods. JB drove past the house, turned, and parked in front. He sat there for a few moments, disturbed by something. It wouldn't sink in right away.

Then the light came on in a section to the left of the stone suto-Elizabethan style house. The place was complete with a sloped overhanging roof. The light was a square of white in the gray of the winter day. JB could see the black cross hatched bottle glass windows that distorted the view into the room. He then looked at the rest of the house. That's when it snapped. There was no picture window.

JB doubted that there had been any major change to this ancient looking house since it was built circa nineteen-eighteen AD according to a bronze plaque by the mail box. JB looked back at the house. This sort of fantasy architecture was considered stately and quaint in that era.

JB went back and sat in the car.

There was no way Theo, sitting in his car that night,

could have seen into the Dean's study as he had testified. He had to have been *in* the house. He had to have been in the murder room to be able to describe the woman's death so horrifically. So detailed. JB bet it was Lionel who was sitting in the car. Made more sense. He was the car guy of the trio.

That was what Ronald and Teddy had on each other. It was what bound them to each other through all the years. True, their partnership made them a great deal of money. But they were held together by ropes tied in Hell. Which one held the gun that night? Which one panicked when the lights came on? Pulled the trigger in surprise? Killed another human being? Was it Ronnie or Theo?

How was JB to figure that out? Only the principals involved could answer the question. And all of them were now dead. JB turned the key in the ignition and headed out of town.

Was it possible Ronald had returned earlier than Osgood the butler said he had. Three days before the funeral was he in Mawahawken? Had an argument with Lionel on the front lawn of Miz Bittie's house sent Ronald over the edge? Was he, angered by Lionel's betrayal, driven to fiddle with Lionel's brakes? The money he sent for all those years to Miz Bittie being old Father Guilt working his rotting fingers on Ronnie's immortal soul.

A silver Chevy with a missing side view mirror was already idling at the stop light ahead when JB pulled up behind him. The light turned green but the car didn't move. It sat there, smoke billowing from its exhaust. Wasn't that sort of pollution supposed to be monitored? Then the light changed back to red. JB hit his horn, then pulled out and up along side the Chevy. The driver's side window was tinted dark so JB could only make out a body in a baseball cap in the driver's seat. He threw the shape the bird. The light turned green again and JB hit the gas to cross the intersection, heading for the on ramp to the Expressway to Manhattan.

The silver Chevy, now behind JB, hit his gas pedal and pulled up behind his car, adjusted his speed, and was right up on the bumper of JB's car. Riding his tail the Chevy again hit the gas. Tires squealed. JB felt a tap from their bumpers colliding. What the hell? JB was forced to speed up. That left the Chevy to pursue him. The Chevy speeded up too, then continued to speed, repeatedly hitting JB's rear end, which made JB go faster to keep the Chevy from damaging his car. Soon both cars were speeding upwards of eighty miles per hour. Could that bruiser of a PI be getting back at JB for besting him in their scuffle? In this stupid and dangerous manner?

JB could see the on ramp for the freeway ahead of him. At the last second JB turned the wheel and raced up the ramp onto the roadway.

The Chevy was left to keep speeding down the city street.

As JB's heart started to slow down he decided that any return to the charms of Mawahawken, even during the summer season, was definitely out of the question.

Twenty Five

Len
and JB were hanging up their overcoats on the rack provided
in the foyer of Lee Arden's apartment. It was a week since
JB had returned from his trip. Receiving an invitation to
one of Lee Arden's famous Christmas parties was a singular
honor. Sort of like being invited to Buckingham Palace for
tea. It meant you were a part of the crowd. Anointed by
Lee's largess into the Broadway community.

JB had on a dark blue Armani suit with a silk shirt
of the same dark blue. A white silk tie splashed down his
chest. Len was wearing tux pants with a gold buttoned
Hunter green velvet coat over a white shirt shot with gold
threads. With a solid gold silk scarf at his neck. He looked
like he was trying for the King Midas of Elves.

"Your missing the curled up shoes. "

"I look fabulous. So shut your hole."

"Feeling a bit acerbic, are we? The ghost of Christmas evil has arrived?"

"I'm nervous, JB. God, I wish I could drink. I hate, hate, hate these kinds of affairs. I hate being on for everyone."

"But, your always on. What so different about this?"

"Its hyper on. Engines revved. The smile needs to be just that much brighter. Your energy that much more shiny. It's exhausting. These sorts of parties always gave me an excuse to drink."

"Which is probably why you weren't invited to any of them there at the end. Just be charming and try not to cut someone's balls off with that Jensui knife tongue of yours. You'll survive just fine. Now, inside." JB pushed his hands in a shoo the geese like motion.

The white apartment, smothered in black a few months before, now had green glittered holly leaves with red berries spread throughout its rooms. Against all the white it made the place almost forest like, exactly the effect the designer had been trying to achieve during the three hours he had worked on it that afternoon. The country-like effect was greatly enhanced by the pine tree that soared up the two stories to the apartment's ceiling. Decorated with hundreds of twinkle lights in blue and purple it was as magical a Christmas setting as JB had ever seen. Women in evening gowns, men in dress suits stood or sat while waiters in short white coats mingled with drink and canapé trays.

And mingling is exactly what JB and Len did too. They greeted friends, found other cast members, got separated, arranged meetings with people in the business. That sort of socializing. Sort of like the annual office party, but dressy.

At one point JB, walking past the television room, found the critic Alexander Woolsey holding court. He was a white haired old twat who had taken a short stint as a critic-at-large for the *Times* and built it into a couple of gossipy books, a weekly newspaper column on a lesser paper, and had even wrangled a lead in one of the trashiest movies of the preceding decade. He was the Miss Muffett of journalism, and would color a column for the sake of a quotable line. His reviews bordered on the outrageous, missing libel only by inches.

Surrounded by acolytes he was expounding his opinion on a recent movie he had seen.

JB stood at the back and listened.

"I just adored *Pretty In Pink*. I think it will go down as one of the most influential films of the Nineteen-eighties."

JB heard himself speaking up.

"Are you kidding, Alexander? Other than a sweetly capable performance from Molly Ringwald that film was pure trash." The crowd on the floor looked from one man to the other. JB went on. "It had a wretched script. The writer cribbed his plot from college romp films out of the Nineteen-thirties. Maybe in twenty years the movie might achieve some sort of camp status, but that's no real distinction. It puts it right up there with *Ma and Pa Kettle* and *Francis The Mule* movies."

People could be heard gasping. Alexander stiffened. He had the same look Queen Victoria used when unamused. Len suddenly appeared at JB's side, grabbed his arm, and steered him out of ear shot of Alexander's reply.

"Are you nuts? You can't throw his bad judgement in his face like that. And who put the humbug up your ass anyway? I want that Jensui knife back."

"I was simply stating an opinion the opposite of his."

"What you were doing was committing social hara-kiri. Had you persisted you could have used the Jensui knife on yourself. Why don't you take your Holly Jolly little butt into that room right over there..." Len pointed to a set of double doors with a pine wreath hanging in the center. "...and give yourself a time out?"

"I was annoyed at his pontificating. Pompous ass."

"As were we all. Go." Len pointed.

Inside the doors was a book lined library. In contrast to the living room this room was dark woods and overstuffed red leather chairs. A white carved marble fireplace dominated the back wall. Rembrandt lighting gave a warm coziness to the room. A Persian carpet softened JB's footsteps. He went to a bar table and mixed himself a Scotch and water. As he was taking a sip he heard Lee Arden say, "I was hoping I could get you alone, JB. I've been meaning to talk with you."

She stood from one of the chairs facing the crackling fire. The room was filled with the scent of the holiday from the pine cones she was burning.

"I didn't realize you were there, Lee. You startled me."

"I'm sorry. JB, why don't you come sit with me? We can have that conversation I was talking about."

"Okay.", he said, hesitation coloring its very utterance. As he went to the chair Lee explained, "I was just sitting here thinking back to other Christmas'. When Teddy was here. And Christopher was a boy."

JB realized it had been, for her, mere weeks since Teddy had died. She was, of course, still the grieving widow. That she had shown the fortitude that she had during these last hectic rehearsal days proved she was the trouper everyone said she was. A professional in every sense of the word. He went over to the chair with his Scotch. As he settled back, she went on. "I think Teddy would be happy with what we've done here. With *Mrs. MacKenzie's Muddle*. Don't you?"

"I think Teddy would be very proud of his son. And of you. All of you have pulled off quite a feat. Literally out of the ashes. Is that what you wanted to talk about?"

She played the gamin. "Don't tease. What I really wanted to ask was about the book you're writing on Teddy."

"You mean the one I did some preliminary research on as a possible project? Don't worry, I decided not to do it."

"But why? Oh, I wish you would, JB."

"Are you sure?"

"Of course. I want the world to know all about Teddy. I want to keep his name alive."

"Lee. Honestly, maybe you should re-think that. Even my bumbling research into Teddy's background brought up some very disturbing things. Things that could implicate him in a major crime. And a thirty-five year old cover-up. Any professional researcher could find out the same thing much faster than I did. That is if you might be thinking of doing a book yourself."

"What are you talking about? You mean Teddy lied about his past?"

"Did you ever actually see any of the movies Teddy was

a dancer in?"

"Yes, of course, he pointed himself out in a number from *The Ziegfeld Follies*. He was in the chorus."

"In a movie made in Nineteen-forty-six? How big was the chorus? Two hundred and fifty? Movie production numbers were huge back then. I'll bet he just pointed to a tiny figure and said it was him. Lee, I'm sorry, he was never in Hollywood. He came here directly from out on Long Island. His real name was Theodore Brewinski. And the show where you met? Your first show? It was his first too. Think back. Was he even familiar with standard dance terms?"

"He had his own language for his steps. I understood him immediantly."

"Of course you did, Lee. You were in love with him. He could tell you anything and you wanted to believe it. Now think again. Do you remember when Ronald Prescott showed up in your lives? Think back to when he took the stage manager job and first met Teddy?"

"Sure. I remember that. A few months after Teddy and I met."

"Was there any sign that the two men might have known each other before then? Some untoward familiarity. Slaps on the butt? That sort of thing."

"Oh, never. Ronald was always so uptight. Even then."

"How about a nickname? One of them using a strange nickname for the other?"

"No. Oh wait. Ronald would sometimes call Teddy a pistol, like it was a nickname. Teddy always told him to stop it, but Ronald kept right on. They almost came to blows over that. It was so silly. It was Ronald thinking Teddy was a real pistol. A go-getter."

Or…was it because Teddy was the one holding the gun that night in the Dean's study?

"Lee, the two of them, Ronald and Teddy, they were partners for a long time."

"Yes, Ronald was always loyal."

"But were they happy with the arrangement?"

"What do you mean. They were business partners."

"So were Gilbert and Sullivan. They hated each other."

"Oh, I see what you mean." She shrugged. "There were shifts in power between them over the years. At the first Ronald seemed to be in charge. Then a couple of years later it was Teddy running the show. After that Ronald always answered to Teddy." She thought a moment. "But that shifted again later still. That happened when Teddy wasn't having hits. That was a bad time. But mostly the partnership worked. It was just the dynamic of the group."

A couple of years she said? Maybe around the time Ronald visited Lionel in Mawahawken? When Ronald tampered with the brakes on Lionel's car? Suppose Teddy knew about that? It would change the dynamic between them, wouldn't it?

JB looked over at Lee. "That would explain the motive in all this. Why Ronald Prescott wanted Teddy gone. Why he murdered him."

Lee slunk back into her chair. "You just said that Ronald murdered Teddy. How? Why?"

"Ronald gave Teddy a tampered with inhaler that afternoon at the last rehearsal. When Teddy took a hit from that inhaler it caused his all ready weak heart to accelerate. It killed him. Why? I suspect, it was Ronald thinking Teddy was going to ruin his production company. Ronald stood to lose millions if Teddy had opened the show he was creating. It would have been a disaster."

Lee didn't look the gamin so much anymore. The businesswoman in her, the one who had let her survive in show business for so many years, was now in her place.

"I knew the show was a total train wreck from watching the rehearsals. And Teddy was getting more and more erratic. His ideas were getting so outlandish. And really sex charged. The ladies from the clubs would have never let it play. Bottom line—those old biddies from New Jersey. The women's groups. They're what's supporting Broadway these days. Without them buying tickets the show wouldn't open. I couldn't let that be his legacy. That mess couldn't be Teddy's last production."

"Wait, Lee, what are you saying. That you had a hand in Teddy's death?"

"No, not exactly. But I could have. You see, I knew something no one else did. I had even sworn the doctors to secrecy." She lowered her voice. "Teddy had a brain tumor. It was going to kill him. They found it when they did his bypass operation." Lee had begun to cry. A single tear ran through her heavy makeup, causing a small rivulet in its powered surface. It was soon followed by others. "That was why Teddy was becoming so strange. Thinking so oddly. It was the effects of the tumor. The doctor's said it was from a blow to the head very early on in his life. It had laid dormant until recently." She dabbed at her eyes and sat straighter in the chair. She picked at a spot on the arm. "So maybe it was a blessing that Teddy died without that awful production being his last show."

"Lee, you've got to stop this. Just because you might wish for something doesn't make it your fault. You can't blame yourself."

Was it possible that a brain injury given to Teddy by the Mawahawken police thirty-five years before had then burst a blood vessel that became a tumor that was making Teddy Brewster destroy his career? Or, could Lee, aware of that—knowing what it would do to Teddy as it continued to grow—have decided to end Teddy's career on her own. To stop him from disintegrating into a vegetable. Would that have been a mercy? Or a murder?

Lee asked, "JB, is that why you went out to Long Island last week?"

"What? How did you know..."

Looking not the least bit guilty she said, "I hired a private detective to follow you."

"You? I'll have you know that guy you hired literally drove me out of town. Unfortunately, I wasn't in his car at the time. " JB went on to explain the maniac behavior of the man when he was leaving Mawahawken. "Why would you hire such a nutcase? And how did you even know where I was?"

"I had no idea he was like that. I found him in the phone book. I'm so sorry. But JB, you were going around questioning everyone about Teddy. And then you wanted to go into his apartment? To get the atmosphere? Come on. Even I got suspicious after that. I wanted to know why you were going out there? I knew where you were because you left your location with Christopher. He told me. So, the PI reported you were asking around about Ronald. And some murder trial. Right? Ronald was from there."

"So was Teddy. They knew each other as high school kids."

"And this terrible thing in Teddy's past happened there. What was it?"

"Lee, believe me, you don't want to know. You can be assured it isn't the story Teddy told you."

She looked at JB for a long moment then sat up straight. "Liberty Valance," she said. There was a finality in her voice. A decision was made. She would brook no other answer.

"What?"

"The movie. *The Man Who Shot Liberty Valance.* The last line. 'When it comes to a choice between the truth and the legend, always go with the legend.'"

JB smiled. "I couldn't agree more completely."

Lee stood. "Would you like some eggnog? I make mine with rum."

❧ ❧ ❧

JB and Len, having reconnoitered, were standing together, drinks in hand, discussing the party milling around them.

"Not the most enlightened group I've ever been around."

"Len, what is it? What have you done? You look like you've eaten a beehive?"

"I just spent the last twenty minutes talking with that man over there." Len pointed at a narrow man in wire rimmed glasses standing by the tree. "Turned out he's a medical researcher at NYU. He talked for fifteen minutes about his scientific theories on the cause of AIDS. You know what's interesting about his theories?"

"What?"

"Nothing."

"You didn't tell him that, did you?"

"Of course not. I simply asked him if he'd found his theories scribbled on the bathroom walls at the CDC. He was saying that the disease was caused by tainted milk brought in from Jamaica. How ridiculous can you get?"

Since the arrival of AIDS in nineteen-eighty-one

every quack and suto-medical man had his own crackpot theory on the origins of the disease. Everything from childhood traumas to pig sweat to green monkeys had been suggested. And because of that confusion shyster pharmaceutical companies were offering "cures" that often included expensive vitamin packets along with meditation and enemas.

"You know, JB, he seemed taken aback when I accused him of witch doctorery. That he was killing people with his idiocy. What a numbskull..."

"Len, you didn't?"

"I did. I told him that even I knew it was HIV that was the cause and he should be hung for espousing anything else."

"You didn't?"

"Then he ran way over there to the other side of the room."

"Which I have to assume was your intention?"

"Of course."

"Well, we've both made our share of enemies tonight haven't we? I'm going to hear about that run-in with Alexander."

"And that sort of jeri-rigged research is going to make gay people really angry. At least it does me. I'm already fed up with this sort of crap. Did you hear what Falwell said? 'Its the wrath of God on us.' For crips sake..."

◈◈◈

"Dahrling!" Betty Kane had made her usual show-stopping entrance. She was arriving late and obviously after attending another open bar soiree somewhere else. JB and Len watched as she air-kissed an acquaintance, then staggered after a waiter carrying a drink tray.

JB said, "Well, that could lead to some interesting confrontations. Maybe we won't get blamed for wreaking the party after all. Just think..." They each felt a hand land on their shoulders.

"Hi, fellas."

They looked and were astounded to find standing behind them, the recently arrested Jimmy Jameson. Or rather the fake Jimmy Jameson. God only knew what his real name was?

"You're out of jail?"

"On bail. They don't have any charges to hold against me anyway."

JB said, "What about the man up in Rochester? The real Jimmy Jameson?"

"He refused to press charges after we met and I got a chance to explain", and he smiled. That smile was one of the reasons the guy kept getting away with his scams. Bright and engaging it could lull one into thinking it was sincere. "And call me Bill. That's my real name after all." At least he managed to look a bit guilty as he said it.

Len hugged him. "Jimmy…I mean Bill. What a surprise. You being here."

"I'm with someone. I'm her date."

"Who's date?" Len asked.

"Not her?", JB said pointing after Betty.

"Yep. I'm with Betty Kane. She posted bail for me."

"Why would she do that?"

"Because I'm her fiancée."

"Do you want to run that by me again?"

"Betty and I started seeing each other after a rehearsal one night a few weeks ago. We're going to get married. As soon as she divorces that Roger guy. And I'm going to get my antique shop, Len. Isn't that terrific?"

Len and JB exchanged looks.

"Yes, how great for you, Bill. Good luck."

A bellow from the next room caught Bill's attention. "That's Betty calling. I'd better go. Good seeing you."

Len waved as Bill scurried toward his call.

"The mistress commands. I think I know who wears the balls in that family."

JB shook his head. "It's the same old con, Len. Different participants…"

Len said, "Definitely different."

"But still the same old grift."

"He'll pay for it this time. Betty won't be anybody's patsy. I almost feel sorry for him."

The party ended about 2AM. JB and Len, in their overcoats, scarf's, and hats walked up Columbus to West End, then over to Fifth Avenue. They walked past the Plaza

Hotel, stopped at Tiffany's to look in the windows, then took in the lights and Christmas displays at Bergdorfs and Saks. Finally they grabbed a cab and rode home together.

◆◆◆

And that was it. JB didn't pursue any more information on Teddy Brewster. Kelly also called it a wash and closed his file on him, assuming, as everyone else did, that the murderer, if there was one, was Ronald Prescott. And that was contingent on if there had actually been a murder committed to begin with. There were those that were convinced Teddy had committed suicide. By sex. Nudge. Nudge. Wink. Wink. Others were just as convinced it was simply a heart attack. JB supposed that the true answer would never be known.

Dance: Ten

Twenty Six

About
four months after New Year's, Nineteen-eighty-seven JB
had a visitor at his apartment one evening.

Mrs. MacKenzie's Muddle had opened on schedule, in
January, and was a bonified hit. Rave reviews. Lines at
the box office. Sold out for months ahead. Len was settling
in for a good long run with the production. He had found
himself a stage actors dream job. A strong part in a hit
show that would run for years.

What he was then finding out, after playing to sold-out
houses for a couple of months, was the almost monastic life
it required of him. One needed to conserve one's energy for
those eight shows of singing and dancing every week. So
Len's life had become the theater and his apartment. Not
much else.

JB had started getting calls from theater producers

to come in and look at their troubled shows. Could he fix it? What should they do? He was now a show doctor to the Broadway theater community. At least on a part-time basis. JB loved the jobs when he got one. They paid well and didn't require a great deal from him, and being in any theater for JB was always a kick. He was working on a new novel too. So he was becoming a bit of a monk himself. Work and the theater gigs filled his time to the brim.

His visitor on that evening was Christopher Brewster. They hadn't kept in touch those last months so JB was pleasantly surprised when he rang. JB buzzed him in, quickly straightened up the apartment, and went to the door.

When JB opened it he was shocked at how Christopher looked. Terrible. This beautiful man now was thin and sallow skinned. His clothes swam on him. He looked old, great bags hung under his eyes, which were red rimmed. And he looked tired. This wasn't good at all. JB was worried by his demeanor as well. He could see clearly that Christopher had suffered some terrible emotional blow. He seemed to be hanging on to the edge of his sanity by his fingertips.

JB reached out for him, took him in his arms, and felt him shutter at his touch. He led Christopher inside and showed him the couch. He barely made a dent in the cushions when he sat. Sitting next to him, JB placed a hand on his leg. It felt bone thin, as if there was no muscle, no fat. This really wasn't good.

"What is it Christopher?" As if he hadn't already figured it out. "Please tell me. What can I do?"

Christopher burst into tears. "I've got it, JB. The AIDS."

That's the way it was talked about in gay circles. With a preposition. *The* AIDS. As if is was some sort of hulking monster, a grim lumbering beast that grabbed you in the middle of the night and spirited you away. In a sense that's exactly what AIDS was. And here it was in reality. In the middle of JB's living room. It was what JB had suspected was the problem. He didn't know anyone who went through such a radical change in only a few months unless there was something drastically wrong.

JB, up until then, had known of several people who

had died from the disease. Hearsay all of them. A friend of a friend. The neighbor from the supermarket. An acquaintance. Someone he had worked with.

But Christopher was the first person that he had really known. That he had been with. In the biblical sense, as bible belters would have it. JB tried to think back to when he and Christopher were getting it on. Had they been safe? He was sure they had been. Was there a chance he was infected? Had he noticed any sores? A cough? Fatigue?

Then JB brought himself up short. What's wrong with you? This isn't your problem. It's Christopher's.

JB looked over at him. Then reached for him again, pulling the sobbing man into his arms.

"I took your advice, JB. I got tested. I'm positive. The doctors said I had to go around and tell all of my sexual partners. So they could get tested too. That's why I'm here, JB."

Of course, JB thought to himself. You'll get yourself checked and that will be the end of it.

"Oh, Christopher, I'm so sorry. I wish there was something I could do."

"There isn't. I'm doomed. I'm going to die, JB. And soon."

To be honest, that was probably true. At that point in the crisis the prognosis was grim for most anyone infected with the virus. Especially at what looked like Christopher's stage. He was a walking target for any infection to take him. Christopher had stopped crying and was wiping at his eyes.

"I can't get my head around this," he said. "Any of it. Everything's been a waste. All the plans."

"Don't say that. You've accomplished so much."

"And it was all for nothing. Teddy dying. The show. All of it. For nothing." He was crying again.

JB was at a loss. He wasn't sure what he was supposed to do here? And what did Christopher mean about the show being a waste? It was a hit?

JB took Christopher's arm, feeling how thin it was he loosened his grip. "What was it supposed to gain you? How about that your contribution to Broadway musical history has already become storied all along the street? It's going to be legendary, Christopher. There will be chapters in books about how you saved this show. Historians will argue motives. Mysteries about its participants will abound. And go unsolved."

"You do make it sound important. And very gay." He snorted.

JB laughed with him. Then said, "About that motive? Why would Teddy's dying be for nothing? You've said he had a heart attack. How could you have planned..." JB stopped.

Christopher, looking at his hands, said, "Teddy's death?"

He looked into JB's eyes.

"Let me explain..."

"How you killed him?" JB assisted.

"It wasn't like that. Teddy wanted to die. I helped him when he couldn't do it himself. I put the amyl in Teddy's inhaler. So he wouldn't know exactly when he would die. He had tried to do it himself. He couldn't."

It all came in a rush after that. As if Christopher was expiating something that had festered inside him.

"You remember I told you that Teddy and I got close when he was in the hospital?" JB nodded. "Well, we did. We got really close. At the end he was the father I had always looked for. And as we talked Teddy came to see my own vision. And he approved. He knew I could carry his torch. Not damage the name. Do you know that he had seen every production I directed? He never let me know he was there. He just came to watch. There in the hospital he knew he was lost. He knew *Mrs. MacKenzie* was a mess. We talked about how if he were fired from the production, how I should step up and take over. Make the show my own. This was after the doctors had found the tumor on his brain. You knew about that, didn't you? Well, he knew the show was a disaster. It wasn't a giant leap from him being fired to him dying. He decided he wanted to kill himself. He tried. With his behavior. Keep the reputation alive, he said. But he was stronger than he knew, and he survived all the abuse he heaped on himself. Finally, he begged me, JB. He wanted me to give him something that would take him out of the hole he was sinking into. Have you ever heard of someone called Kavorkian? He's a doctor in Detroit. There was an article he wrote recently. Advocating death with dignity. The man makes sense. So, I helped my father to end his life. And one of the reasons he did it was to give me a career. And that is now nothing."

JB then told Christopher another side to Teddy's story. How his death was perhaps retribution for a crime committed even before Christopher was alive. How both Teddy and Ronald's lives were stolen, ruined by the sins of their long ago pasts.

There was nothing to be done about Christopher's culpability in Teddy's death. His own death was going to be far too obvious payback.

JB would file this one under great stories I will only tell my closest friends. And then only after everyone is dead. How long would that be? How many years? What is the lifespan of a Broadway star? For it was Lee Arden that would suffer the most in this. JB was thinking Len could be of great help for Lee. They had become close friends since rehearsals.

JB, after brewing a fresh pot of coffee, sat with Christopher and told him about a group he was working with. Called GMHC. Gay Men's Health Crisis. They had resources that could help him. JB also volunteered to be Christopher's buddy. He explained that was a program started by the group to help men infected with AIDS. He would visit and do whatever was needed for Christopher. Chores. Meals. Shoulders for the tears. They could take this last journey together.

Christopher pulled himself together and thanked him, hugged him, and said he had to see someone else that night. He promised he would contact the group JB had mentioned. And he left.

JB never saw him alive again

About the author

Ken Lansdowne has lived in California, Nevada, New York City, New Mexico, and now lives in Denver Colorado.

The first novel in *The Bent Mystery* series is *Secrets Don't Belong In Closets*, the beginning. Second is *A Murderous Ball of Fluff.* Third is *The Fairy Dust Killer.* Fourth is *Home Sweet HoMo.* Fifth is *Dance:Ten Murder:Maybe?.* Sixth is *A Mystery, Wrapped In A Mystery, Surrounded By A Mystery.* Seventh is *The Art Of Death,* and number eight is *Bathhouse Bloodbath!*

There is also a Gay themed Christmas novella: *Jacob Marley*

If you would like to get an automatic e-mail when the next book in the series is ready for release sign up at k.lansd@outlook.com. Simply put the word "LIST" in the subject line of your email. Your e-mail address will never be shared and you can unsubscribe at any time.

Word-of-mouth is crucial for any author to succeed. If you enjoyed the book please consider leaving an online review, even if it is only a line or two: it would make all the difference and would be very much appreciated. If you didn't like it I apologize for taking up your time: my purpose was only to entertain or give you a laugh or two.